Acceptance:

The Beginning

Rebecca Heidt

Copyright Page

This book is a work of fiction. Names, characters, places, and incidents either are the product of the author's imagination or are used fictitiously. Any resemblance to actual

persons, living or dead, events, or locales is coincidental.

Edited by: Brianna Fredriksen

Synopsis Written by: Tatianna Mason

Cover by: Arash Jahani

Dedication Page

∞

I dedicate this book to all of the humans that are dealing with all the emotions of life. This is for those struggling to heal and are struggling to find their way through the fog. You are heard, you are seen, and are loved. Keep moving forward, no matter what comes. You got this.

A special dedication to several individuals for their support:

Kevin Heidt

James Heidt

Jo-Ann Messer

Irwing Nieto

Prologue:

Acceptance was a word that I learned in school. We knew how to say it, how to use it in a sentence, and its meaning. For me, though, I took it as acceptance that I was the sole person in control of my future. My willingness to be obedient of what was asked of me, keep control of my emotions, and accept that I had a burden to bear, a secret. Acceptance that I have a duty to uphold to my family. To keep calm.

To each person, this word means something else. How could one word hold so much meaning? Little did I know what that word would mean to me.

I am Selena Wilson. I grew up in Stockholm, Sweden, raised by my Uncle, Liam Wilson. It has been him and me for as long as I can remember. I don't know a lot about my parents. Uncle Liam never opened up about it. All I know is that they died in an accident. I never knew what they looked like. There were no pictures of anyone around the house, ever. Uncle never explained the detail of the incident to me, and there was no information I could find on the subject in any public records.

Uncle had us live a simple life. He believed in helping people less fortunate than us and protecting living things. His head is shaved at all times. He wears a basic brown tunic with sneakers, which I have told him is poor fashion sense. But he doesn't seem to care what people think of him. He runs a natural medicine shop on the first floor of a building in the city's center. Along the back wall of the store, a door led to a spare room. Usually locked, this room possesses an open area for a practice space or storage. A separate entrance along the back wall leads to stairs up to our living area above the shop's location.

Uncle didn't care for worldly things when it came to living and did not allow electronics into the house. The only form of electronic entertainment we had was a radio. He believed that my imagination was enough. Uncle built my life around puzzles of all kinds, meaning to keep my mind sharp and teach me patience. When I solved a mystery, my reward was the radio.

My childhood, from what I saw of other families, was an unusual one. Growing up, my Uncle taught me that I was not the same as other children. I would have episodes, he called them, when I lost my temper or felt a feeling too strongly. These "episodes" usually led me to show a brute strength that was beyond my age.

These experiences are why Uncle trained me to channel the feelings into something more productive. Instead of causing destruction and punching concrete walls, I could learn to defend myself while helping others in need. Two nights a week, along with the weekends, he would teach me the art of battle. I learned hand to hand combat, swords, and daggers. Having these unique qualities as a person and with this

* * *

upbringing made it hard for me to make friends. Especially as a child watching other kids having a different life and talk about the current fashion or trends. I couldn't talk about the same topics.

They thought I was weird, which made me stick to myself.

Then, in middle school, I met Melanie.

I was eating alone. Melanie just started there, moving recently to the area. She got a tray of food from the line, looked around, and walked straight over to me. She set her tray down across from me and just started talking.

"Got anything fun there to eat? It looks like a sandwich, blueberries, and a cookie. No drink?" she surveys my area in front of me and grabs one of her two cartons of milk, "want one of mine?"

I stare at her outstretched arm with the milk before responding, "I don't drink milk."

Melanie looks confused, "You don't drink milk? What do you use for your cereal?"

I shrug and pick at my sandwich, "I eat cereal dry in a bowl."

She giggles, putting the milk back on her tray, "That's weird. You're different, but I think it's cool."

I smile a genuine smile at her. She starts eating her meal, "I'm Melanie, but I think you know that because you are in some of my classes. You're Selena, right?" I nod my head. "Will you show me around town later?"

I take a bite of my sandwich and look at her. I use this time chewing to assess this girl who is trying to embed herself into my life. She is waiting for an answer from me. I nod my head again, "Alright."

After that first conversation, Melanie and I were best friends. Uncle accepted her into our lives as quickly as I did. With the understanding that I could never tell her why our experiences were so different than hers.

As I grew up, Uncle continued to train me. To be observant, aware of my actions, and respond with precision. With adulthood came the time for me to branch out on my own. But Uncle always kept a guiding hand and a watchful eye.

Chapter 1:

A blade swings just above my head. I can hear the swishing of it and feel the air after the edge passes my face. I duck on instinct. We are in the practice room in the back that only the two of us have seen. The room has bare walls with no decorations adorning it, except burning incense, a mirror, and a mural on a wall panel. The mural is a painting of a tree blossoming pink flowers by a small pond. The incense's smoke is slowly curling in front of it. I am unsure if the sandalwood incense's smell calms me or annoys me after all the years.

There are foam mats on the floor, our bare feet moving across them. Uncle is in his brown tunic, as always. I'm in yoga pants and a t-shirt. My breath is coming out forcefully; it always seems more ragged than his when we practice.

My hands grip the handle harder, but I relax my stance.

Ready at a moment's notice, my muscles will respond. He swings first, and I immediately move, our swords clashing. It is all about who is faster. I dodge a swing to my stomach by a couple of inches. Well, I guess faster and more controlled really. The arm muscles start to burn with the effort from my tight nit movements. Neither opponent is ahead of the other. Ten actions later, we end with a scene that's a tie. Each sword snuggly placed against each other's necks.

"Are we done with this game now?" I ask with an even, stoic face.

Internally, my pride smiles because I know I am getting better. The point though is not to show it too much; that would just lead to lecturing. But guessing by the holding pattern we are in, this is not one of the areas requiring coaching.

Uncle holds his skilled hand in place, unmoving, looking me in the eyes. "I know you are older now, but that doesn't mean you know everything. The second you think you know everything will be the moment someone will get the drop on you. Always keep learning." He says, his voice not giving anything away.

Apparently, I was wrong about not needing coaching.

I keep my gaze level with my Uncle's, a smile slightly presenting itself, not daring to move until he relents. His face is tough to read. I can't tell if he is upset or proud.

"Hmm," is the only noise he gives me before lowering his weapon to his side. I match his movement and lower my arm as well. As soon as my weapon is down, he reacts by lunging towards me. I respond immediately by blocking. Grabbing his arm, I twist it to force the weapon out of his hand. Once the blade falls, I end up putting him in an arm hold against the wall. I effectively disable him and return my weapon to his throat with the point pushed up under his chin.

He gives a short laugh, "Yes, now that you have beaten me, we are done for tonight." I let him go out of the stance stepping back. "Just because you won one fight doesn't mean you will win every fight."

I return my weapon to its position on the wall, then shut the cabinet doors, "No, it doesn't, but as this is my first win, I will remember this day forever."

"As will I," he smiles at me, "the rest of the night is yours as you wish after you help clean up."

I help him pick up the mats. Together we fold them to fit in their usual spot against the wall. I jog over to put out the incense safely, then store them in their container. Uncle comes up next to me and shoos me away.

"Thank you, Uncle," I bow to him just like after every other practice in my life. Then run out of the room before he changes his mind.

"Don't break anything!" He yells after me. I roll my eyes but smile. His dry humor is not lost on me.

"Been there done that!" I yell back to him while putting my socks, shoes, and jacket back on to return to the world outside this building.

My Uncle's shop long since put behind me. I travel home to change with a couple of hours to myself. Even though it is still cold from the winter months, I crack my windows open to let the breeze into my apartment. This breeze gave a hint of a promise of things to come.

I slip a ring on my right hand with the knowledge that with the new season comes change. I shake my head, smirking at myself, wondering what the warmer weather would bring this year.

I slide the other ring onto where it belongs, feeling the change start through me for the first time in a while. It is similar to a wave going through one's body and settling down, the feeling of adventure, a journey ahead of you. Even with all the promise of the possible fun this feeling is sending, there is a phantom. It is a lingering of an unknown sadness and loss.

This has been happening for more than a couple of years to me. The loss does not have a concrete reason or event attached to it. The knowledge of it always slipping to the edges of my consciousness. Now that I am older, I have just barely begun to understand the basics of what this change is and why I feel something vibrant but missing from my soul.

The mirror shows back what I already know. My brown wavy hair remains close to perfect. My hazel eyes are already shining, mischievous, and playful. The look is attached with a lingering smile trying to escape from its depths. I leave the room with a bounce in each step that I feel through my whole body, a crackle of energy that almost feels tangent. On my way to exiting my rented building, I grab some small daggers to hide away just in case. After my home is locked up tight, I take a deep breath in and out. Keep calm and controlled, I think. I start to move with no set destination in mind, just to enjoy the night out in my favorite city.

⁕ ⁕ ⁕

I wander around, finding myself in one of my favorite spots by the museum. I end up sitting on one of the benches along the water. Sometimes when I have some free time while it is not yet dark out, I will look out over the water horizon to think. To enjoy people watching and observe the sky turn to pink with a hue of orange, marveling at the universe. At times I feel that if this action is not completed, I will lose my mind. It is referred to as a grounding exercise, or so I am told.

I watch as old colored leaves float around with the light breeze still lingering in the air. They are showing the wind being playful with the earth to the visible eye. The scene is one that inspires creativity and serenity to the mind.

By now, there are not many people around, with it being later in the day. Families are most likely home or out eating dinner. Several couples walk hand in hand in different spots around the museum. There are even fewer individual people leaning against the railing looking out around them, similar to myself. I wonder if they do this for the same reasons I do, looking for all their answers in the wistful air. I take a second to observe the other faces. I can see looks that show concentration and thoughtfulness in some kind of form across their features. Seeing this makes me smile from getting my answer, knowing I'm not alone in this sense.

I move off the bench from the waterfront to avoid getting stuck in my thoughts for too long. I have to get ready for work after all. The temperature is starting to lower as the sun disappears. I hug my jacket slightly more closely to me. I set my navigation towards the metro station. On the way, I pass an older woman who is strolling and seems unsteady. I stop for a second to check on her.

"Hi there. Are you doing okay?" I ask the older woman.

She looks over at me and smiles, "Oh, hello there. Yes, I am okay just trying to get a taxi to go home. Would you help me to the curb bench?"

I look up from where we are and see the area she is talking about half a parking lot away, "Yes ma'am, I can." I entwine our arms and amble over with her.

The woman continues with small talk, "It's such a nice day out that I couldn't pass it up. But I am not as agile as I once was, and my feet hurt."

I softly chuckle at her openness, "It is a lovely day out today. I am glad you get to enjoy it."

As we reach the bench, she pats my arm, "Thank you honey, for the help." She lets go of my arm taking her temporary spot.

"Sure thing. You have a good night." I turn to leave as I see the taxi lights approaching against the dusky sky. I continue my walk towards my destination away from the museum.

I then hear a distressing female voice.

"Wait! That's my taxi!"

I turn to look where the older woman was sitting a moment ago, seeing a man opening the car's door to start entering it. I immediately begin to move towards them, running.

"Hey!" I shout, "That isn't for you!" I get there fast enough to stand in front of the door before he can close it.

He looks at me baffled, "Where did you come from?"

"Your conscious. Get out, or I'll make you get out." I put my hand on his wrist, which remains still on the door handle.

"No, I need this taxi. I am in a hurry. She can call a different one," the man says, trying to close the door with my body still in the way.

I take a deep breath that turns into a deep sigh. "Option number two then."

With my right hand still on his wrist, I reach in with my left, grabbing the front of his shirt. I squeeze his wrist to let go of the door. Then pull his entire being out of the car. I toss him on the sidewalk next to the bench—the look of surprise very present on his face.

I give him my annoyed face, "Find a different way home."

At this point, the older woman has gotten up from the bench to stand more behind me. The man stands up, brushing himself off. His anger is starting to come to the surface from the ordeal. "I don't know who the hell you think you are, but you have no right to do that," he half yells at me.

I step closer to him, and he backs up the same amount, mirroring me, "Similar to how you don't have the right to take advantage of people? You don't get to hurt people and not expect consequences. Get out of here!"

He doesn't move right away and just stares at me. I take a step closer with more aggression, "Now!"

He jumps at my tone and runs away towards the inner-city lights. I let out a slow breath to keep calm. That could have gotten out of hand quickly. I look around me to assess the situation. The cab driver is just staring at me open-mouthed. The older woman is smiling at me next to the open door. Maybe I put it on a little heavy.

I clear my throat to try to diffuse the awkward aftermath, "You are all set for your cab now, ma'am."

She moves to hug me, "You are just so lovely. Thank you so much for helping me tonight! That was incredible."

I just stand there, letting her hug me not moving, "Uhm, you're welcome. I need to get going though. Have a better night." She lets go of me, pats my arm again, and gets into the cab. She starts shutting the door. As it is closing, I hear her reprimanding the driver that it's not nice to stare and to shut his mouth before bugs fly in.

Chapter: 2

After getting home, my thoughts wander to the interaction with the weird guy and the older lady. The situation made me feel a little off. Similar to a feeling of overstepping boundaries. But regardless of how I felt, I needed to let it go. The situation already happened; there was nothing I could do to change it now. My priority right now is getting ready for work mentally and physically.

Since I am more of a night person, I had a stable job as a bartender at a local establishment, Joe's. The name is not very original, but the owner is caring and pays decently. He pays me more because I always help keep the peace when things get a little crazy with the drinking crowd. It's not a very fancy place, just like any other bar. It has a small stage for live bands or karaoke and is the house to two pool tables for groups to enjoy.

A bar's success is typically base upon the types and variety of music playing, the staff's friendliness, and the types of drinks they make. We are lucky to have all of those things, which provide us a good customer base.

The earlier interaction at the park puts me behind schedule. I don't own a vehicle myself and didn't have time to walk or take public transportation today. Quickly, I call Melanie to see if she can give me a ride to work.

The phone rings, and she answers on the third note. "What up biznitch, what's crackle a lacken?" Mel asks immediately.

"Still alive as of today, same problems different day. I'm working at the bar tonight and am wondering if you could pick me up?"

"Yeah, girl I got you," then she hangs up.

I remove the phone from the spot against my ear, staring at it. Why does she do that? I roll my eyes and start getting changed for work.

Roughly thirty minutes later, I am attempting to tame my hair into some kind of normalcy in the bathroom when someone bursts in through my front door. I instantly go for my dagger, stored in the small of my back.

"Selena, are you ready?" reaches my ears as I am about to throw it. I quickly alter the course to land the dagger safely into the wall a foot away.

"Jesus, what have I told you about entering my home without prior announcement? I could have injured you!" I say, showing my exasperation.

"Either way, you get in my face thinking I'm someone who is going to hurt you, so I figure I need to go big or go home. Though I did not expect the artillery." My best friend responds with a small chuckle and a smile. She seems rather chipper for having a sharp object thrown at her.

I strut up to her and push her lightly on the shoulder, "Mel, you are so lucky you are my best friend. In fact, my only friend. I could have killed you on the spot. Next time knock and use a code word."

She rolls her eyes and folds her hands over her chest, "The only thing I am going to say out of that is thanks for not killing me…and my code word is You-Are-An-Ass," she says, leaving the apartment to go to her car. I grab my keys, the dagger from the wall and casually leave after her. Hopping into the passenger seat, I buckle in and shut the door.

"I am okay with that code word," I respond after getting settled and wink at her.

She sighs, shifting the car into gear and says, "You're lucky I like you so much even with all your trauma drama," then speeds off down the road.

The short trip with Melanie is occupied with random thoughts she has and me smiling in response and offering the occasional shake of my head. The beauty of Mel is that she has allowed me the space to see what everyday life is supposed to be, while giving me the space to act and be myself without a million questions. Melanie knew from our long friendship that I'm not the same but never put pressure on me about it. She lets me talk about what I want to, when I need to. If my friend noticed something not quite right in a scenario, she would only lift her eyebrows and smile in acknowledgment. But she has never once interrogated me during our friendship. I look over at her, still talking. I'm lucky she chose me to sit with those many years ago.

"Are you even listening to me?" Melanie asks me in a disbelieving tone.

"Yes, you were running on talking about your crush on Brandon," I say as I turn to look out the window at the passing scenery.

"No, I was talking about my crush on Benjamin," there is a pause, "Brandon is my ex now."

I chuckle. "Of course he is. I was technically not wrong."

"Don't laugh at my love life! At least I have one. What about you? When are you going to start dating?"

"I am not ready yet. From what I've seen, it's a lot of effort to put into another person. I need to keep working on myself before putting my problems on others. When I'm ready, I will know."

She pats my knee as she pulls up to my place of work. She parks then squares her shoulders towards me. "It's okay. When you are ready, I will impatiently be waiting to hear all about it.

Now get out and get to work." I laugh heartily at her statement, thanking her for taking me, and shut the car door. I turn around to head towards the bar entrance, and I move quickly to arrive on time. I go to the machine to clock in and start my normal process to get ready for the night rush.

The night turns out to be a very calm, stress-free night, though Wednesday's usually are. I stand behind the bar, cleaning glasses and look at the clock. It's showing 1 am with about an hour until close.

My boss Joe comes up beside me and starts to clean glasses with me. "If you want, Selena, I can finish up by myself. I know you have things to do."

"You sure, Joe? I don't mind. You won't have me to help you until Friday."

He smiles at me fondly, "Nah, I'm good I can handle it."

I glance around the partly occupied room, noticing mostly full glasses, patrons actively conversing, and shrug. I stop what I'm doing and get ready to leave. Clocking out, I tell Joe not to miss me too much, which is our regular good-bye.

Chapter: 3

After work, I decided to walk the long way home instead of taking any form of transportation. I am feeling rejuvenated. My soul is in the mood for fresh air, feeling charged with flowing energy. My attitude is calm, like the thoughts in my mind regardless of what is happening outside in the current world.

I walk along the streets, taking in the scenes laid out in front of me with each step, each block. I'm taking in the random lights of apartments that are still awake at this hour and the quietness that stretches out across the night air. It has a peacefulness to it, a serenity that is disrupted by another soft pair of feet on the pavement.

They are not very loud but noticeable enough for me to lose focus on my observation of the streets. From the steps' sound, they are going about the same speed as me, if not a bit faster. This was a person whose attention was solely on me. If it weren't, then they would be going at a different speed of pace. Either faster to pass or slower to stay an extended distance from me. Not roughly the same length, continuously keeping me in front of them.

The person behind me has the advantage point right now. The only element I have on my side is coming up with a plan to surprise them.

Then I hear another pair of steps out of sync with the first. The second pair is slightly more hurried either due to distance to catch up or height difference. I am estimating that I am half the distance to my apartment. I don't want to lead them to my home. Uncle's shop is nearby to here, but I don't want them around him either. I need to get them away from the area. Let's test these people.

I turn right onto the next street and start to walk faster. I hear their steps turn right as well but farther behind. Yeah, that's what I thought. It's time to get creative.

I turn right again on the next street and break out into a sprint. Halfway down the block, I switch to the opposite side of the road. I hear my human shadows start running once they realize they are about to lose me. I turn left, running straight down the block towards an apartment complex. I need to get the upper hand. When I get there, I hide on a small hill behind a trash disposal unit.

Thirty seconds later, I hear a male voice out of breath in a harsh whisper say to his partner, "She's here somewhere. Look over there. Find her."

A figure comes around towards the front of the trash disposal unit. I get ready to jump down towards the figure. I see a guy dressed in black cargo pants and a black long sleeve shirt. His back is turned to me, looking around the paved surfaces. I take that second to jump on his back. He is startled and starts trying to get me off. I put my legs around his waist and my arms around his head in a sleeper hold. He can't get a good grip on me and starts slowing down. He falls to his knees while I land on my feet to keep the hold in place. He slumps forward, and I lay him on the ground.

I pick up the top half of his unconscious body and began to drag him off the walkway. I want to minimize the alarm as much as possible. A passed-out human on the ground would cause a lot of questions. I have successfully placed him around the grass hill when I hear running steps close to me. I turn around quickly to see what is going on. That is when I get football tackled in the stomach by the second person.

I quickly surmised two things. One, this man is dressed the same as the first one. Second, this man is the larger of the two from my assessment of body types. He hits me like a ton of bricks. I am confident that when I hit the grass, my skin has grass stains from the force.

With the wind knocked out of me, I elbow him in the back several times until he lets go. His grip loosens on me. This allows me to roll away from him and get my defense in place.

We both stand up and square off to each other. Who I am squaring off with is the guy from the taxi fiasco.

"You have got to be kidding me! Of course, it's you. You got problems, man. Why are you so weird?" I say to him incredulously.

"The only problem I have is with you. He will be excited to talk to you."

"This sounds like more weirdness. I don't want to talk to anyone that is in connection to you."

I must have hurt his feeling because he lunges at me. I'm ready this time, sidestepping him. He expertly uses his momentum to turn back towards me, putting out a punch. I block it immediately. We do a little dance of punches, blocks, and kicks. He is well versed in fighting, enough to hold his own. I fake punch with my left, which he falls for, and punch him squarely in the ribs with my right balled fist. He doubles over in pain, either from a bruised or broken rib. The pause in time allows me to land a solid kick to his chest, virtually eliminating him as an immediate threat.

It takes me all of five seconds to decide to run past this played out scene. I move quickly to make sure these guys' don't tail me to my house. Uncle was not going to be very happy about this development tonight. But my main priority right now is to get home and get some rest.

When I reach my home, I'm out of breath from all the running. I slam the door behind me and lean against it. What a night! More than I would have liked to have dealt with. My mind and body are completely drained. Trudging to my bed, I leave a line of boots and clothes.

Once becoming comfortable, sleep soon overtakes me.

There is black all around me. I reach out to feel my way around the darkness. My hands lightly brush on some skin. I try to zoom out through my mind's eyes to see what I'm touching. Or should I say who I am touching? This action feels so foreign but so intimately familiar. I have determined that based on the familiarity, this occurred before. In an unknown time and place. Is this a memory or a dream?

My hands find themselves in silky hair, but the color of it keeps changing. Feelings of all kinds swell inside me. This feeling doesn't seem to only originate from my heart, but my whole being, my soul. It feels like a yearning, a love, completeness. These emotions are unfamiliar to me. I put defenses in the way to stop this vulnerability from ever becoming a weakness. These defenses I put up don't feel as strong as I expect. They are feeble at best. Either from their efforts to break through or from my lack of conviction.

This person who is under my fingers has figured out what no one ever could, how to get close to me. Who is this person? I feel the edges of my mind pulling, trying harder to find the answers to my questions, to my fears and confusion.

My eyes snap open to a knock at the door.

Someone's here.

My favorite sweatshirt is nearby. I groggily throw it over my head and stumble over some discarded shoes. A curse

* * *

lingers over my lips as I grab the handle and open the door. My right eye remains shut in my sleepy state, and my left braces against the sun pouring in. I open it only to find no one standing at the door.

Crap, now was I dreaming it, or is someone messing with me?

Well, let's be honest sometimes I dream crazy things. Like that one time, I dreamt I punched someone and ended up punching myself in the face. I shake my head.

Yeah, like that.

Chapter: 4

After an impressive start to the morning, my main and only goal is to visit Uncle's shop to fill him in on what happened. Entering through the front door, I set off the beeping security alarm, which announces my arrival. I walk past organized shelves of different themed medical herbs. Accessories range from calming effects to remedies for headaches, and I notice him working on a table near the counter with his back to me. I weave through the different shelves and tables to Uncle, who is in the process of stocking some tables, yawning.

He continues organizing the table, "You seem a little out of sorts today. Everything okay?"

I pick up an object to fiddle with it in an absentminded manner, "Just tired. I had some weird dreams last night.

Though something odd did happen yesterday that I need to tell you about."

Uncle stops what he is doing, turning his shoulders to face me. He gave me his full attention, "I'm listening."

Replacing the item I'm fidgeting with, my eyes meet his in respect, "There was an incident with a guy and an elderly woman that caused me to step in to help. Later last night, after work, he and an acquaintance tried to jump me, follow me, or something like that. I shook them off, but it wasn't normal."

Uncle seems to soak the information in, his face thoughtful, "Why do you think they were trying to follow you? What makes you think the behavior was out of the ordinary?"

I'm tilting my head in thought, details playing back in my mind from the night before. The fight, the dream after, really none of it was typical. "The guys were wearing the same black clothes, and the guy knew how to hold his own in a fight. He mentioned a person being excited to talk to me. Which made me think that they were trying to kidnap me."

Uncle frowns, seeming deeply perturbed, "Did he say anything about the person further to indicate who it is?"

I squint at him slightly, unable to keep the sarcasm out of my voice, "It is not like we had a ton of time to stop and chat about his vague statement."

My snarky remark did not phase Uncle at all. He pushes on with his line of questioning, "Did you give yourself away at all?" I sigh, "No, I didn't show any of my abilities other than the fighting, winning, and running away."

He nods, satisfied by my answer, "You need to keep a watchful eye out now that someone seems to have you on their radar. Be on your guard. There are things in the store I need to get done today. Come back later tonight for our training session."

I start moving towards the door feeling a bit annoyed, giving him two thumbs up, "I am always on my guard. That is how you taught me. I'll see you later." As I exit the building that held most of my childhood and youth, I can feel his eyes on my back. Similar to the sun burning its heat rays against one's clothes on a clear day.

I go back to my place as I wait for time to move forward for our training session. I had no plans for the day other than to relax. Sitting in my usual awkward position in my chair, I begin tossing my dagger back and forth. This is the closest to relaxing that exists for me.

My mind goes to what the two of us discussed earlier. This existence that Uncle wants me to live can be so distrusting and paranoid. I understand it is for our safety, but it can be hard sometimes. Is this a way to live? In the dark? Away from everyone? He taught me to help people in need but from afar. He always told me not to get involved in other people's issues.

Maybe this is why though. People are jumping you in the middle of the night because you hurt their feelings. When you take control away from others, they act out and hurt people.

● ● ●

I sigh, always so complicated. What if I had a normal life? Was born in a different family? If I were someone else, it would be boring that I am sure of. But if I didn't know better, it probably would have been enough. And thinking about these things will never change the situation, but the possibilities remain interesting.

These weekly thinking fests are just a routine for my quiet time away from my reality's chaos. They both make me smile and break my heart at the same time. The Ying and the Yang I do not let anyone else see.

After several hours of self-contemplation, the training session is due to start. Upon returning to Uncle's shop, I walk in and over to the Buddha Statue behind the counter. There are candles all alight in front of it, as well as around the sides. The Statue is glowing from the illumination, causing a peaceful site. I immediately sit on a cushion, Indian style. I am relaxing as much as possible.

Uncle taught me before entering the backroom to let go of all the bad energy. The faster my body could relax and let the stress go, the faster I could go home to sleep.

Uncle is kneeled in front of me, leveled with me holding my shoulders softly. "Remember Selena, you are different than other girls and have to be careful. You need to be in control all the time." he reminded me again after another incident.

"What if I can't keep control, I don't want to hurt people."

"Well, my dear, when the time comes, you might have to hurt people. You were given a gift, but it is also a curse. To protect yourself, you may need to try harder." The smell of incense lulls me closer to sleep, along with the sound of his voice. "You will have to meditate every day to control your emotions to keep others safe. You can't come to see me until you are calm. You must follow this rule; do you understand my child?"

"Yes, Uncle"

I open my eyes. I feel as ready as I can be to see him and start our session.

Chapter: 5

I am in the back-training room, making sure I am ready to face him by taking off my shoes, socks, and jacket like I always do. Uncle has not spoken to me since I have come in. He doesn't always talk to me when I join him, but this time seems different. He finishes lighting the incense, the mats are already down, and I wait for him.

Uncle walks over to the corner of the room where there is a cloth covering something. He takes the fabric off to reveal two spears. I raise my eyebrows in surprise. We haven't spent time going over spears before. He grabs one and tosses it to me. I catch it midair, and he immediately lunges for me. The spearhead directed towards my upper chest.

I react to his action by going to block the metal tip. I push his advance up over my head. I scaled back his attack, or I thought, but he brings the end of the spear to hit me across the cheek. It is just hard enough to hurt, maybe leave a bruise. He moves the end that recently connected to my face in a downward motion aiming for my foot. I move my foot away as his weapon hits the spot where I was a moment ago. I take that second to use the middle of my spear to push against his, making him move back.

We both circle each other looking for the next move. Uncle expertly twirls the spear around him.

"What are you upset about?" he asks as he keeps circling the mats with me.

"I'm not upset about anything. We are training like we always do," although the response is said, my eyes are keeping a watch on his footwork and arm movements.

"You aren't telling the truth. You are holding something back. What are you upset about?" Uncle goes to the offense with several weak forward movements. He's watching my reactions to each.

I block him by volleying his attacks in the direction away from me, "I don't understand what you are trying to get at."

"My question is very straightforward. What are you upset about?" Every time he asks, it is in the same tone of voice. It starts to make me feel agitated.

I take a deep breath and make my move. I fake an advance out towards him. When he blocks it, my spear's opposite end is knocked perpendicular to the floor closest to my feet. I kick the end towards him, which hits him in the stomach. He moves back then immediately proceeds forward for the gain over me. Uncle does a sweep against the floor with the spear aiming for my feet. I jump over, and he twirls with the momentum. He uses the movement to hit me with the blunt end. We do several more jabs and blocks between us with the spear staff before we both step back to reset our stances— slightly out of breath.

"You haven't answered my question. What are you upset about?" Uncle repeats before standing the spear on the floor next to him.

I match his stance, "I have answered the questioned, just not the way you wanted me to."

As soon as I answer, he moves his spear, swinging it forward, hitting my spear out of my hands. It clatters to the floor a short distance from me. He addresses me by putting more authority in his words, "You need to address what is going on, or it will be harmful farther down the road. What are you upset about?"

I immediately set my eyes sternly on him. He waits for an answer that doesn't come. The next advance he makes is the sharp end of the spear coming at me. I duck under the weapon. When I rise, I grab the middle of the wooden spear and twirl away from him. This action easily dislodges it from his grasp. When it is removed from his hands, my palm heel strikes his chest—causing him to stumble back.

I point the spearhead at him, "What I'm upset about is that I am suspicious and guarded with everyone. I live a life of darkness! Hiding all the time is exhausting! I am certain I wasn't born to live a life so secluded. I can't talk to my parents about it because they aren't here, and you won't talk about them. I don't know what I am here to do, but this couldn't be it."

Uncle moves closer to the spear tip, letting it push against his stomach as he puts his hand over mine, "Look in the mirror Selena."

I turn my face to the mirror on the wall. What I see is my face, but my eyes have a hue of green to them. I lost some of my control, and it is showing. I failed my training today. Even though I won the fight, I forgot all my teachings' central concept: Don't lose control. I bring the spear to a resting place by my side. I give Uncle an apologetic look.

His eyes rest on me with a wisdom beyond my years, "I know our way is not always easy, Selena. You want to be like normal people, but you aren't. Just because you are different doesn't mean you are less of a person though. I am here to teach you to survive and win in life. My main priority is always to keep you safe." He reaches for the spear in my hand to remove it and puts his hand on my shoulder. "You are everything to me. Dwelling on what happened to your parents won't help you build your future. It will only hold you back."

I nod my head, then look again in the mirror, my eyes back to a normal color. I feel some regret for putting Uncle through all of this. He has done the best he can to protect me from myself and others.

● ● ●

My gaze turns from the mirror back to the man who raised me, "But why am I so different? I feel like I am missing a piece of important information."

His eyes do not waiver from my own even though the conversation is on a sensitive subject that we don't often discuss, "Some answers I just can't give you. But, if your questions were answered, would it change anything? Would it change how our life is now or how you conduct yourself?"

Uncle's questions weigh heavy in my mind and chest. Would knowing about my parents change anything right now? The air remains silent as I think over what he said.

My eyes return to his, "No. I don't think the answer would change the way I do anything right now."

He walks over and picks up the other spear, "I think that is enough training for tonight, Selena. Go ahead and head out. I'll clean up tonight."

I bow to him out of respect, "I am sorry, Uncle."

He bows back with a sad smile on his face, "They are things that needed to be said."

Uncle starts to organize the room while I get ready to leave. Once outside the building, I let out a long breath. I look back at the building that gives me so much comfort and heartache at the same time.

I stop by my work for a quick drink before heading home. I hang out at the edge of the bar. I don't want to bring too much attention to myself. I'm not here for a social call.

Joe sees me shortly after arriving and gives me a look. I am sure my emotional exhaustion shows on my face. He pours me a shot of vodka and puts it in front of me. I raise it in a small toast to him, then toss it back. It burns in my throat and on its way down to my stomach. A feeling that I welcome right now. I slide the glass back over to Joe, moving to get money from my wallet. He shakes his head. I give him a salute of thanks as I stand up to leave. I push through the doorway to the outside world to head home.

My inner dialogue is running wild. I needed to accept that I would never have the same things or experiences as other people. But it seemed more problematic for me to be okay with that the older I got.

My eyes survey the people in the area around me with wariness. Uncle did the best he could with what he had, making sure I could be self-sufficient. I could survive and hold my own against those two guys the night before because of what he taught me. My perception of normal should be more dependent on situational awareness. The fact was my situation was unique, so my perception of normal was also unique. I watch a couple fighting outside a café as I passed on the other side of the street. It doesn't seem like anybody knows what normal is anyway.

Chapter: 6

The next day is my favorite day of the week, Friday. People are more carefree, there is a lot more excitement, and they give up more money when I serve them. I always go to work earlier, prepping for the busy rushes and sporadic groups of customers.

As usual, I'm behind the bar getting drinks that are requested and laying on the charm. Faces are coming in and out of view of my bar top. There are always new faces that came through here, and then there are the regulars whose names I knew.

It's a standard Friday night at work, except in the sense that it isn't. Some of the new faces today are somehow different than the clientele that typically comes in.

There seems to be one guy in particular. He keeps coming up to get a variety of drinks for his buddies. It's not his large bill that piques my interest; it's the way he looks at me. I know that customers find me attractive and try to hit on me, but it's the intensity of the look. His gaze is not of the superficial kind; it's the kind that wants to know all your secrets. The expression is him showing interest without pushing me. I guess it reminds me a lot of how I am.

When I first saw him, he came up to get a pitcher of beer for his party. Before he even cracked a smile, I could tell he had some issues. The type of clothes one wears and how they present themselves says a lot that words can't. The way he holds himself is telling me he has some dark shadows behind him, giving off the air that he is not a pushover.

He's wearing black boots, blue jeans, a red t-shirt, and a leather jacket. From a closer look at the leather, it says he came from money. Enough people watching has shown me a leather jacket is not just a style but a statement. I find that relatable on many different levels.

His hair is sandy brown and short with a clean-cut look. Even though his hair is short, it's debatably the second-best aspect of the snap image I take of him. The first aspect being his eyes, which are hazel with a mix of amber. Unusual eyes for what I could only guess is a unique person.

When I hand him the pitcher of beer, he smiles his gratitude and asks for it to be put on his tab. With that, he turns and walks back to the previous company he was keeping.

● ● ●

However, I am surprised; he did not try to talk me up or hit on me like the guys and girls usually do in a bar.

My attention turns back to the other customers, flashing on the smiles and laying out the drinks. There is a woman who's waving at me—leaning over the counter, a flirty smile on her face.

When I reach her, I match her smile, grabbing a clean glass, "What can I get you, hon?"

"A Molten Sunset, please."

"Sure, you got it," I look over at her, and the girl's eyes are traveling up and down my body, checking me out. I softly laugh to myself. This woman is a very open type. Noticing this, I put more energy into swinging my hips and exaggerating my movements. By the time the drink is going on the counter, she has money out to pay for it.

I take it to ring her out when she speaks up, "That's all for you, gorgeous. Thanks for the show," She takes the drink and sips on it.

Before she walks away, I give her a wink and huge smile, "Any time, doll."

The guy in the leather jacket comes back to the counter as she leaves. His group did not last long with the pitcher. The next order is several beer bottles and some shots. Some of the party-goers branch off and play pool.

I notice that more or less the same people stay around the guy in question, in constant conversation. By the fourth trip up to me, we have barely had any conversations except necessary friendly interaction, so I decided to give in a little.

He approaches the counter smiling at me. When I'm within earshot, he asks, "Can I please have a round of Bourbon shots and a pitcher of beer?"

"Sure thing," As I get the shot glasses, I ask him, "You and your buddies celebrating?"

He smiles wider at me and leans on the counter with his arms crossed over each other, "Something like that. I came up with an excellent idea at work and got promoted for my dedication."

"Must have been one heck of an idea for that to happen. Congratulations are in order." I hand over the pitcher of beer, a tray of shots and look around the place. All the other patrons, at the moment, are busy with their own entertainment. So before he leaves, I call out to him, "Hey, since you seem to be a genius, that pitcher of beer is on us tonight."

His smile returns to his face, and he lets out a small laugh, "Thanks."

Before there is a chance for further conversation, I turn away from him to check on the dirty empty glasses cluttering the bar top. My rule is to be nice to people but not allow them to get too close. This guy acts like me a little, which causes me to want to know him more, but I need to be careful how close I get.

* * *

Before the night is over, he closes out his tab and leaves me a large tip. I am only slightly surprised by this, considering he clearly has money. His buddies were getting ready to go, some of them steadier than the others.

"By the way, my name is Ryder," he grabs a napkin nearby and writes something down, "This is my number. I hope you'll call me to talk more, away from all this." He waves around the bar at his friends before handing me the napkin.

"Thank you. I'll think about it." I respond as I put the napkin in my pocket.

"Good enough for me." With that, he turns around and ushers the group towards the door.

I watch him leave the establishment, and I continue cleaning up. It's not like I haven't gotten numbers before, from both girls and guys. Usually, I would never end up calling them. I never felt a reason to before. But a different part of me wants to call Ryder.

Maybe I'll talk to Melanie about it. She has only been waiting for this our entire friendship. I call Melanie and let her know I'd be on my way over shortly after closing.

Chapter: 7

As I approach Melanie's place, I train my eyes on the window of her apartment. I'm not sure how I want to bring this up without being awkward. Melanie is the only one I have to talk to about this. Being without my parents left me with little knowledge in specific areas that my Uncle Liam could only help with to a small extent. This happened to be one of the subjects I did not feel comfortable broaching with him.

I went straight to where the balconies start a floor below Melanie's. I climb up the first one and reach for the bars to her balcony. I move with skill and grace to the window that looks like any other, but I know it is different. Out of boredom, my initials ended up in the window frame one random night. I tap on the window with my ring, making a sharp noise to contrast the night.

"Yo, Melanie, let me in," I harshly whisper through the glass.

She comes into view, and I can't help but give a smile coupled with a small wave. She comes to open her window to her two-bedroom apartment.

"Are you literally ever going to use the door? Like you have a spare key and everything," She chastises me as she moves to give me room through. She may outwardly object to my entering this way, but I know she finds it funny deep down.

I shrug, "Probably not," then smile wide, "I like to keep some traditions alive."

Melanie just shakes her head and ushers me further into the apartment.

"What are you up to?" I ask as casually as possible as I look around. The TV is playing, and a table lamp illuminates its rays to show me that she has several coloring pencils scattered around a coloring book about nature. She only colors when her brain won't shut off.

She walks over to her couch to resume her place and picks up her coloring book. She continues whatever coloring section she was working on before I disrupted her evening, "I'm watching a show about a western demon hunter and coloring. I just found this show. It is utterly amazing; you should watch it with me."

I walk over to the other couch and lay down with my legs hanging over the armrest, "Cool, cool, cool." I let the room fill with the sound of the show as I stare at the TV.

Without looking at me, she starts the conversation, "You don't' usually visit me on Friday nights. You seem a little off tonight, is everything okay?"

"Yeah, of course, I'm okay! While I was working, someone did give me their number, though."

She nods her head as she colors, giving me only part of her attention, "I am unsurprised by this. It's not new for you to have this happen. I imagine you would be used to that by now."

"Yes, you are correct. The difference is that I'm thinking about calling this one back," I respond as naturally as possible.

Melanie stops coloring mid-page, "What did you just say?"

I clear my throat to dispel my anxiety, "I thought about calling him back tomorrow to meet up at some point."

Melanie squeals her excitement while jumping up off the couch. Causing the coloring book and pencils to fall to the ground, "Oh my god! I have been waiting for this our entire friendship!"

Her statement causes me to laugh since I already knew that. She comes over to me and sits next to me on the floor, facing me. The coloring is long forgotten, "Tell me everything."

I shrug, "There's nothing to tell. His name is Ryder, and he gave me his number."

Melanie is staring at my face with a thoughtful look, "That is pretty basic information. So, you don't know anything about him as a person. Why do you want to call this one out of all the other ones?"

I take a slow, steady breath and look at her, "He reminds me of myself in some ways."

She nods her head thinking about what I just said, "Okay, normally not something you say. I can get behind that. Since you know virtually nothing about him, just be careful."

I give her a knowing look, "You know me, Mel, I am a fountain of careful. My every step is well calculated and precise."

Melanie softly pats my leg from her place on the floor, "Sometimes you need help. You can't always do it on your own."

Her statement hits a soft spot in my armor. It touches on insecurities that come around once in a while, mostly on my bad days. My eyes float to her gentle, supportive smile. I match her small smile in acknowledgment of her statement. And naturally, ignore it completely.

I nod my head in the direction of the show still playing, "How about we watch some of this show you are so excited about?"

Melanie proceeds to get up and grabs her discarded pencils, launching into an explanation about the show. She goes to the guide of the program to start it from episode one.

Chapter: 8

The next morning arrives, or rather the afternoon, since Melanie and I stayed up so late together. When I feel like my brain and senses are operating like an average person, I pull out Ryder's number to give him a call. The other end starts to ring, and the feeling of anxiety starts to rise. What if he doesn't answer and I have to leave a voicemail? Should I leave one? If I did, what the hell would I say? Three rings in, the thought of hanging up weighs heavier in my chest. The noise suddenly stops; I hear a voice say, "Hello?" Oh, he answered.

"Hi Ryder, this is Selena from last night. From the bar. You told me to give you a call."

"Oh hey, Selena. I am glad you called. I'm about to walk into an impromptu work meeting, but I was hoping to see if you want to meet up for dinner later tonight."

I stand up and start pacing, "I don't normally eat dinner. What about a café for coffee and a brunch?"

I can hear his laughter on the other end of the line, "Don't eat dinner? That is hard to imagine, but I would be okay with meeting up at a café. Say…two hours from now? Text me the name of the place, and I'll be there."

My jittery behavior causes my eyes to roam around the room while he's talking, lacking focus on any one particular thing, "Okay, sounds great. I'll see you in two hours."

A couple of hours later, I find him outside the café waiting for me. He is wearing jeans, a green pullover sweater that has the zipper open showing a nice black polo underneath. When he sees me, he smiles his appreciation and lays on the charm, "You look nice."

"Thank you. Ready to go get a seat?" I'm hungrier than I want to admit and need to get my order in now before the small talk begins.

After entering, the employee ushers us to a two-person table. Even though it is the weekend and lunchtime, they take care of us right away. Our waiter comes over soon after to get our drink order and see if we are ready to place our meal order. I end up getting a coffee and a sandwich, Ryder a tea, and a salad. After placing the orders, Ryder collects my menu from me and hands them over. It's then left to the two of us at the table to entertain each other.

He moves more to the edge of his seat, keeping his back straight and one forearm on the tabletop. He seems like he is trying to relax but is too tense to make it happen. As I watch him, he looks around at the architecture before noticing me observing him.

Locking his eyes on me, he opens the floor for conversation, "This is a different café. I've never been here before. Do you come here a lot?"

"No, this is my first time here too. I always wanted to try it. There were a lot of great things said about it, and I figured it was worth checking out."

"You ordered pretty quick then considering," Ryder retorts. The statement confuses me, and it must have shown on my face. He explains further, "the company I usually eat with would have taken a much longer time, no matter the restaurant."

His statement makes me laugh outright before retorting, "Most café menus are similar to each other with small ingredient changes and a couple of their signature creations. It comes down to mood, I suppose."

Mid conversation, he looks around the surrounding area back and forth, almost absent-mindedly saying, "I wonder where our drinks are."

He is trying to see through other people to behind the counter where they make the beverages. I look at him with doubt, "Hmm, probably making the coffee I ordered. It has only been maybe a couple of minutes."

Ryder stops trying to look behind the counter when I say this to him. His attention is now back to me, turning his body, sitting squarely in the chair. He smiles apologetically, letting out a small laugh, "I'm being controlling, aren't I?"

I smile back at his receptiveness to my previous statement, tilting my head slightly, "Controlling. I'm not so sure about that, but pushy? I little bit yes."

"Sorry about that, I am just used to being that way because of my job," As he says this, the waiter arrives with our drinks placing them in front of us, "Ah, here we are! Thank you!"

The waiter places the coffee in front of me. I raise it closer to my nose, taking a second to take in the scent—a hint of vanilla mixed in with the coffee grounds. A genuine smile reaches my face. As I blow on it, I take a moment to look up at Ryder, adding sugar to his tea. He looks like a quirky kind of guy. Strong-willed, straight forward, demanding, and a little weird. I test the delicious beverage for temperature by sipping it, taking a second of enjoyment to myself.

As I set the drink back in a spot near me, a small tentative smile plays on my face, "So Ryder, what do you do for your job? It sounds like you are very good at it."

Ryder immediately beams emphatically, answering the question, "The company I work for is family-owned. My parents bought it from the previous owners to help it become the successful business it is known as today. I have recently been taking over more responsibilities from my dad. With him getting older, he wants to take more time to himself. We still have tough competition in our industry, but I am confident with my ideas we will become the top."

"That's pretty positive. How sure are you that your ideas are going to work?" I ask before taking another drink of my coffee.

A smile spreads across his face at this question, seemly excited to discuss this topic in more detail. He comfortably leans back in the chair before answering, "No idea is foolproof. The only thing you can do is try different ideas, as the ideas play out, monitor what results happen as it is happening in real-time. Then make changes when needed."

Both my eyebrows raise at his honest answer. His answer is observant and well thought out. The confidence level was a bit high, but impressive. "You seem like you know what you are talking about. It all makes sense to me. Change what you can when needed and react proactively to what you can't."

Ryder is now leaning against the back of his chair, no longer semi-defensive and on edge. The smile is still there but not as large as when he first answered. His fingertips are drumming lightly on the tabletop. Ryder has a look that I could not identify right away, but it seems thoughtful.

He leans forward and points his finger at me as if he is departing life-altering advice to me, "That is exactly correct. You understand what it takes to win."

I laugh at his answer and how serious he is taking this entire conversation, "What I understand is how to adapt to a changing environment and still come out the other side."

• • •

"Hmm. The truth is that not everyone does," Ryder speaks matter-of-factly.

"Not everyone does what?" I ask without pause. I see our waiter holding two dishes in his hands, which makes me assume they are ours—one of the dishes visibly being a salad.

Ryder answers right before the waiter reaches our table, "Not everyone comes out the other side."

This statement causes me to look back at him quickly. The message he just said can mean many different things. It can be a statement of observation. It can be a statement that he is ruthless and cuts his enemies down, making sure they don't make it. It can be a statement from an empathy standpoint rooted in regret for not helping others make it through their struggles. It is not easy to read what he means since he has already moved on to greeting the waiter with a smile and thanking them for the meals.

The waiter asks if we need anything else, and with the response being a unanimous no, leaves us to dig into our meals. We fall into a temporary cocoon of silence, enjoying our respective selections before continuing the conversation. My attention between the fries and the sandwich makes me aware that this meal is what I needed today.

As I take the second bite of my sandwich, Ryder starts his line of questioning towards me, "What about you, Selena? I know you work as a bartender. Do you have any other things you like to do? Any other ambitions?"

"Not really. I actually like working at the bar. I get to see different people and make decent money. My main goal is to keep working on myself and make sure I don't make the world more difficult than it already is."

While answering, Ryder stops a fork full of salad midair to his mouth, "That's…...an interesting point of view," he pauses several seconds to contemplate something, "What about your family? You haven't said much about them."

I keep my face as unchanged as possible, "There isn't much to say about them. It is just my Uncle and me."

Typically when I say this, people say something with sympathy or empathy. Rarely do they ask what happened to them. I keep this topic as vague as possible for several reasons. Because I barely know myself, and I don't particularly appreciate talking about it.

You can imagine my surprise when Ryder asks me the next question: "What happened to them? Are they still alive?"

When he asks it, I'm aware my face visibly portrays my shock. I watch him shake his head out of whatever mental state he was in when going with that line of questioning. He clears his throat to buy him some time to backtrack slightly from the awkward silence that fell between us.

He tries again, "I didn't mean for that to come out like that, so unfeeling. What I meant to say is I'm sorry to hear that was the situation you grew up with."

I decide to go with a generic answer that would avoid further questioning, "Thank you, it is what it is. There is nothing that could be done to change it."

He continues with similar questions, "Have you lived here your entire life?"

His questions were making me tense up a bit. I once again stick to generic answers, "For the most part, enough that I consider this my home."

Ryder is staring at me, probably trying to analyze my rather vague answers about my family and upbringing. I expect him to get frustrated by it.

Instead, he smiles warmly, "You seem to have a good head on your shoulders. I think a lot of people that work around me would certainly like you. Next week we are holding a gala event with investors to help promote the faces of the company."

A look of amusement crosses my face, "By helping promote the faces of the company do you mean getting the investors to do more investing?"

He lets a deep laugh escape his chest, "Yes, you certainly have an eye for these things. As it stands, I don't have a guest for me to escort to this event. Would you like to accompany me that evening? I would like to see you again after this if I haven't offended you too much already."

To me, his question comes out of the left field. Even though he is upfront with his conversation, I feel a need to gauge his seriousness, "You haven't offended me. But are you sure you want me as your guest to a gala? It sounds pretty important, and you haven't known me for a very long time."

Ryder waves the waiter down to come over to the table. As the waiter approaches, he gives me a smile that lights up his eyes, "I can understand your surprise at the question. Honestly, I could not think of anyone else better to join me at this gala besides you. Having spent more time with you now." The waiter arrives as Ryder takes out his wallet, "Can you please get us boxes and charge everything to this card?" The waiter nods, taking his card from him and walking away.

I blink several times, trying to deal with what is happening right now—looking down at my half-eaten sandwich and fries. I guess I am having leftovers later. The waiter returns with the boxes and hands one to me. Then gives Ryder the receipt to sign. I put my remaining food in the small box.

As Ryder is settling the receipt, he looks up at me for a second, "I need to get going. Otherwise, I would stay longer to talk with you. Unfortunately, I need to work on further plans today that are due in a short time frame. But before I leave, I need to know, will you come with me to the event?" "Yes," I answer as I finish organizing my things.

"Great, I can't wait! It is next Saturday. I will text you the address and time. I must get going, but I had a lot of fun today with you. I'm glad you called."

We get up at the same time to gather ourselves. Ryder comes over to my side of the table, takes my hand, and kisses the top of it, "I'll talk to you later." With that, he heads for the door. As he exits, his phone rings. A black car is already waiting outside for him. He is talking on his phone, paying no mind to anything or anyone else.

I walk out of the café, watching the black car leave. I have zero clothes for this gala event. Shopping is going to be required. That means I need to contact Melanie for assistance, which I'm sure will require very little persuading. Taking out my phone, I go to her name and text her.

Me: Mel, meet me downtown for some shopping in 1 hour at that one store that you love. I'll explain when you get there.

Her response comes back in less than a minute.

Melanie: An impromptu shopping trip? Yes, please!

What the hell did I just get myself into?

Chapter: 9

I find myself sitting on a bench, waiting for Melanie to meet me. She had texted me; she was still five minutes away ten minutes ago. When Melanie says five minutes, it essentially means fifteen. Just add ten to whatever number she says.

I am good at casual events, but when it comes to fancier looks and styles, that's Melanie's area. Diving into a situation I'm not familiar with causes me to be anxious. My fingers are tapping the bench side to keep me distracted from spiraling in my thoughts.

I hear my phone go off, and I check it. The message is from Ryder. Opening it, I find the information about next Saturday's event. He sent the address, the start time being at 7 pm, and an added note that he couldn't wait to see me there. He even put a smiling emoji face. I stare at my screen for a little bit deciding if I want to text back or just leave it alone.

That is how Melanie finds me.

* * *

"Why are you staring at your phone like that?" I hear her voice approaching me from the right.

My head lifts away from the screen to look in her direction, "Like what?"

"Like you are lost or angry. Both are very similar expressions for you, and it's not easy to tell at a glance."

I lock my phone screen before standing up to meet her face to face, "I was thinking about what I wanted to do."

Melanie looks confused, "With your phone?"

I give her a half-smile; she's trying so hard right now. This conversation may take a second. I half sit on the bench arm. With my phone still sitting in my hand, I rest it and my hand on top of my leg. "With a text message I got. I wasn't sure if I wanted to respond or not, so I'm thinking about it."

"Oh! I can help with that. Tell me what's going on, and I'll let you know what you should do."

I shrugged, "It's Ryder."

She slightly leans forward, anticipating more information that doesn't come. When she figures out, I'm not adding more onto that; a sigh leaves her. Her hands firmly on her hips, she asks, "Why can't you give me all the information at once? Why do I have to pry it out of you?"

My fingers start tapping the phone on my leg, "Because that's who I am."

● ● ●

Melanie weighs what I said by moving her head side to side, "That's true. Tell me more, please."

"Ryder invited me to his work event. He wants me to meet his coworkers. It's a nice event, and I need a dress. He just texted me the information to the occasion."

She immediately jumps in to start her questioning, "Did you meet up with him already?"

"Yes, right before I texted you about shopping."

She raises her eyebrows, "After that, he invited you to a super fancy work thing?" I nod in response, "That is a bit…fast."

"Well, I agreed to it, so here we are."

Melanie claps her hands together, "Okay then. Concerning the text you mentioned, you don't owe him anything. You don't need to text him anything, but he is probably looking for confirmation that you are going. A simple response like "Okay" or something confirming your attendance is sufficient. With that being said, let's go shopping!" She moves towards the first storefront.

I hop off the bench arm to follow after her. Before entering the store, I unlock my phone screen to respond to Ryder's text.

Me: See you there.

After, I move to my main screen, lock it, and put it in my pocket—time to try some dresses.

About an hour and ten dresses later, I find myself ushered into a fitting room stall. Never in my life did I ever think that I'd have a conversation about different colors complimenting skin tones.

I start changing into the first one when I hear Melanie's voice drift over the door, "So tell me about Ryder."

The dress settles over my head onto my limbs before I answer her question, "Well, he's knowledgeable, intelligent, pushy, and charming. I can't tell yet if he is controlling or just likes things a particular way. From what I have seen, he knows what he wants and goes for it. He also doesn't seem very embarrassed about it."

I adjust the dress to look more presentable before stepping out. Melanie is sitting in a chair in the fitting area, looking at her phone.

She looks up when she hears the door opening, "Oh, that's cute and sexy! But maybe too much for a work gathering with a guy you barely know. Try the next one." I return to the room to switch over to dress number two as she continues analyzing Ryder's character, "He sounds ambitious, which can be great or a horrible thing."

"How can it be bad?" I ask, half distracted.

"It depends on what is driving the ambitions that make it dangerous. The longer you are around Ryder, the more clearly he will show you which one it is. Believe me, I know from experience."

● ● ●

I step out of my safety area once again to show off my second dress. Melanie delivers her swift judgment, "The color is great but not that specific style on you. Next dress, please." I roll my eyes.

Turning around back into the small unit of space, I go to the next styles. Out of the pile, I choose the color I like most and start to change, "Ryder told me his family is in charge of their own business, and he is starting to take it over. So he is ambitious and competitive from what I've seen so far. His mind seems extremely strategic. He also appeared preoccupied and impatient."

"It's a good thing you got an invite to this then. You will see him in the element he knows best and how he treats people below him. I know you said he is similar to you, and that's why you wanted to meet up. I just want to remind you that sometimes someone can be similar but not fit with who you are or what you need."

From my fitting room, the concern in her voice is evident. She is trying to protect me. This is amusing because I am usually the protector.

"Mel, firstly, your concern for my safety is deeply touching." Melanie took that second to snort a laugh because out of the two of us, our roles in this conversation are usually opposite,
"Secondly, I have only been on one semi date with Ryder. There is no commitment between us. He is almost as guarded as I am. The closer I get to him, the more I will see if he keeps up a front for me. One evening will give me what I need."

There is a pause before she answers, "Yeah, it sounds like you got this covered."

I walk out of the room to show her my choice. She lights up immediately, "That's the dress! Great color, gorgeous, classy but sexy. Forget the rest of them. This dress is the one girl."

Relief flows through me, looking back to the enormous pile of dresses waiting for their turn to be worn. Shopping for a long time makes me uncomfortable. Also, I like this one best and am happy with how it looks.

Melanie stands up from her chair to stretch, "Go change back into normal clothes so we can start looking at shoes and accessories."

I half show my excitement, which probably comes out as anxiety, "Yay." Shoes and accessories that should be fast, right?

Chapter: 10

My time shopping with Melanie was fun but exhausting. Who knew there were so many different shops for everything, but I'm feeling good about the choices we made. As the days continue, my anxiety and excitement slowly increase.

Luckily, I have my work to distract me.

My life activities allow time to move quickly from one day to another. And before I know it, I find myself working my Wednesday night shift. I'm pleasantly surprised that the evening is busier than usual. An influx of tourists always accompanies the warming season.

As I'm finishing a drink order for a lovely Canadian couple, I hear my phone go off. I sanitize the bar top before taking a second between patrons to look at it.

Ryder: Are you free tonight? I want to see you again.

Me: Can't, working tonight

Ryder: Ok, see you soon

I didn't have a ton of time to think about what he meant by that, so I leave it alone—quickly returning to my tasks.

After several more customer orders, I take a second to look around the room, gauging everyone and anything that needs to be done. I thought I saw a familiar face in my sweep, but he was talking to a couple of people farther away, preoccupied, not allowing me to see his face. The uncertainty didn't weigh too much on me.

My attention is quickly taken up by a man currently waving at me. He kindly lets two females order drinks before him and patiently waits for his turn.

"I was hoping you didn't forget about me," he said.

"Not at all. How could I forget someone who shows such kindness to others," I replied quickly to him. The guy beams at my compliment.

"I appreciate it. Can I have a gin and tonic, please?"

"For my new favorite person? Absolutely." I answer, matching his smile.

I move to make the drink like it's second nature to me. Over the clinking of the ice in the glass, I call over to him.

"Does my favorite person have a name?"

"Conner."

"Well, it's nice to meet you Conner. Are you from the area? I haven't seen you before," I ask, putting the finishing touches on his drink.

"No, I'm just visiting. I always wanted to come here for vacation."

I smile wide, placing the drink in front of him. "In that case, we are glad to have you here."

"Thank you," he picks up the drink to take a sip of it before continuing, "This is a great tasting drink. You made it well."

His response makes me laugh harder than I probably should, "It pretty much has two ingredients in it, Conner, but thank you anyway. I'll take it."

Conner lightly laughs with me. I don't know if he's laughing because of how funny I find what he said or because he finds his joke amusing.

"You have a great smile," Conner says.

"She sure does," a second voice says, entering the conversation before I can answer.

My eyes look over to who is talking at the same time as Conner's. The face I find is Ryder, showcasing a smug smile.

"Hey Ryder, I thought I saw you earlier. I guess this is what you meant by "See you soon"," I say, annoyed by his interruption.

Ryder opens his mouth to respond to my comment, but Conner beats him to it, getting my attention first.

"I can see you are about to be busy," he says as he grabs his wallet from his pants pocket. Pulling out a bill, he hands it to me before continuing, "Here's for your impeccable skills. It is all for you."

Taking the bill from his hand, I see it is about double the drinks price. From my brief interaction with Conner, he seems polite, kind, and generally good-hearted. Now apparently, generosity is put on the list as well. As I take the money from him, I give Conner my biggest smile.

"Thank you, Conner, for the compliments and great conversation."

Conner winks at me before taking another sip from his glass and moves away from the counter. Ryder moves to the spot right in front of me, where Conner was previously.

Ryder's smile is still in place. His body is partially leaning on the counter, demanding all my attention.

"You do, though, you know? Have a great smile," he says.

Even with my slight annoyance at him, I can't help but smile more. Flattery will get you everywhere.

"Thank you, Ryder. What brings you here tonight?" I ask.

"I told you, I wanted to see you again," he states bluntly.

I look at him, slightly confused, "Aren't we seeing each other on Saturday?"

"Yes, we are. But I wanted to see you before that, so here I am."

I listen to Ryder explaining himself. He seems to be calculated but spontaneous, selfish but caring, and confident but tentative. I can't tell if I genuinely like him or just tolerate him. But he is trying, and I should probably cut him some slack.

"Yes, here you are," I tilt my head slightly, "Did you want a drink?"

Ryder looks pleased that I asked, "I'll take a Rum and Coke." "Coming right up."

When I give him the glass, he asks me, "Are you excited about Saturday?"

I look at him as he takes a drink of his dark liquid, not answering right away. He seems to want me to mold into his hands and be overjoyed by this apparent gift he's given me. But mainly, I'm just more curious.

When I'm ready, I respond "I'm not entirely sure what to expect. So, I suppose yes, I'm excited but waiting to see what happens too."

His usually happy demeanor falls slightly. I evidently did not answer the way he wanted me to. What is he looking for? For me to gush over him? If he is looking for someone to jump headfirst into this, he chose to invite the wrong person.

Ryder asks, "What do you mean you don't know what to expect?" He pauses briefly but continues, not giving me the time to answer, "There isn't much of a difference between the gala and where we are now. There will be people standing around talking, music in the background, and alcohol to drink. But the alcohol will be free, and everyone will be better dressed."

As I'm standing here listening to Ryder, I know I have to get back to work before I got behind. But I need to ask this question before walking away from him.

"Why did you invite me to this Ryder?"

His usual smile returns to his face, "Because I thought you'd make the evening slightly less boring. Plus, I am amazing. What better way to see what I can do than seeing me in live-action?" he says.

Ryder's answer isn't a bad one. The problem with it is that he is the boss of the party. His job that evening will be to entertain people enough to invest in his business. The whole night will be about him. As he shows borderline narcissism, I can't see him being that bored the entire night. Which is why I'm pretty confident he only said that answer to appease me.

I look into Ryder's eyes before I ask again, "I have to get back to work. Before I do, I'm going to ask again. Why did you invite me to this when at the time, you had known me for all of 10 hours?"

After saying this, there's a brief stare down between us. Both of us are waiting for the other to do or say anything. A simple conversation is transforming into something that is in a league of its own. I'm challenging Ryder's fake charming answer, and he is challenging me to accept what he is saying.

Ryder breaks eye contact first, taking a deep breath. He looks into his glass for several seconds. I glance around the room, seeing several people moving towards me to get drinks.

Ryder looks up into my eyes again to answer me, "Because you get it. I am the one in charge of this business and this party on Saturday. But, you get what it takes."

His answer is straight to the point and seems honest enough. It seems he feels like the other people around him don't get the burden of what needs to be done. Ryder thinks I do and can relate to what he deals with based on our first conversation.

I move away from him, giving him my best smile, "I'll see you on Saturday, Ryder."

Other patrons are waiting to get my attention, but I watch him out of the corner of my eye. He isn't smiling or frowning; his face remains neutral. He appears to be looking into his glass again. Looking for something that the liquid is not going to tell him.

Ryder downs the rest of the beverage then turns around and leaves. The only thing left to show that he was there at all is the now empty glass.

Chapter: 11

After Ryder leaves my work that night, he doesn't call or come back to visit. I don't think much, figuring he was probably busy finishing up details of the event. He expressed wanting to see me that night but seemed to leave more frustrated than he came. What I have seen of Ryder's character is that he expects conversations to go in his favor then gets upset when they don't. This work party will hopefully shine some light on that.

The night of the gala event arrives, and it is time to get ready. Melanie gives me some suggestions on the hair and make-up, matching her whole theme: classy but sexy. Following most of her instructions, I modify the make-up slightly to fit my style more. Before leaving to make my appearance, I take a second to meditate and center myself. No extra emotions need to come on a trip with me to such uncharted territory.

Acceptance: The Beginning

Growing up in a surrounding that did not have material things, it is odd that I'm pampering myself now. I feel out of my element. This whole experience is only highlighting that things couldn't remain the same forever. But just because things as you know it changes, your morals and character did not have to. Feeling more prepared for what is to come tonight, I leave waiting to see what the night brings me.

By the time I get to the party, it is slightly after 7 pm. Several couples are entering the building, discussing essential things amongst themselves. I enter, exhibiting confidence and smiling. There is a mirror on the wall a small distance from the entrance. I stop to take a quick self-assessment.

I'm wearing a dark blue silk gown with a small slit on the side up to my calf. It is tight enough to be graceful but loose enough to do some fighting moves as a last resort if needed. I am wearing shoes that are basic silver heels. My hair is half-up, held up by two silver butterfly clips. The jewelry is matching decorations of silver and sapphire. My makeup is simple: mascara, black eyeliner, white and blue eye shadow, and soft red lipstick. The mirror image is definitely a reflection that this is the most elegant I have ever looked.

"Checking yourself out? If you say yes, then I won't feel so bad doing it myself," I hear the male voice over all the din from the surrounding chatter of the room.

I look in the mirror to the reflection slightly behind mine and break out in a smile.

Ryder's hair is well-groomed like always. He is wearing a suit of black pants, jacket, and tie with a contrasting red shirt. The look is elegant for the evening yet simple.

"As your guest Ryder, I reserve the right to make sure I am good enough for the title," I answer, our eyes still on each other through the mirror.

He takes my right hand in his and kisses me on the cheek, "Don't worry dear, no one else in this room would win out next to you."

After Ryder kisses my cheek, I force a smile. I am not a fan of him calling me "dear". The word rubs me the wrong way.

He takes us to the grand staircase of the elegant building. As we slowly walk down the stairs, I take in how beautiful it all looks.

The stairs and handrail are made of white marble. The columns holding the railing in place have spirals of inlaid floral designs and vines. We are walking on the same deep red carpet from the front hallway. It cascades down the stairs like a waterfall. Upon further inspection, the carpet also has different floral designs in grey, gold, brown, and a lighter green. At the end of the railings sits a statue on each side, a woman and a man, roughly three feet tall. After the figures, the carpet changes into a more vibrant gold color reaching its fingers out into the other rooms.

* * *

Upon our feet touching the bottom of the stairs, Ryder walks to a nearby waiter with a platter of glasses full of bubbly looking drinks. As he moves to the waiter's position, he seems overly confident and I scowl slightly. His behavior appears pushy and precocious.

He is an okay person from what I have seen, but his behavior toward me tonight seems different than when we met before. What is it that I'm seeing? Ownership? Condescending tone? My agitation bubbles at the possibility that he thinks he owns me in any kind of sense. I have to clench my hands, take a deep breath, and unclench. I center my emotions and put on my entertainment face, neutral but amused. He returns with two glasses, handing me one. The charm is coming off him in waves.

He holds up his glass to make a toast between us, "Here is to having the most beautiful woman in the room allow me the grace of being her companion tonight. To you, my dear," after saying that, he knocks our glasses together with a clink.

"Thank you for the kind words, Ryder. Also, thank you for the invite to this event."

I drink some of the liquid from the glass to show respect. Ryder looks very pleased with my compliments. It reminds me of talking sweetly to a bird, causing them to puff up their feather in pride.

Right then, a silver-haired man in a tux comes up to Ryder showing a large amount of excitement. Excitement or too much alcohol, which one isn't clear.

"Ryder, it is so lovely to see you again. How are our investments doing?"

Ryder takes the time to give this man his full attention, squaring his shoulders to him, placing me slightly behind him. He affectionately places his hand on the man's shoulder. I deem him "Silver Fox".

"Edwin, it is great to see you again," Ryder puts down his glass on a nearby tabletop, "I am glad you asked. We are looking into some great new opportunities in different sectors…"

As soon as Ryder said the word sectors, my eyes roll mentally. With him droning on about business and investments, I look around the room. Everyone I set my sights on is dressed nicely in a spectrum of different colors. Some of the patrons were animatedly talking to others around them, some were holding their drinks for dear life, and others looked bored. Just like the colors of their clothes, there is a variety of emotions happening across the floor.

"Oh, Ryder, forgive me, who is this lovely lady you have with you?" Edwin "Silver Fox" asks mid-conversation. My eyes flick back to the two men near me. Both of whom were now looking at me.

Ryder moves his hand behind my back, pushing me forward slightly. He puts me directly next to him before he responds,

"Edwin, may I introduce you to my guest this evening, Selena."

I smile large and put out my right hand for him, "It is nice to meet you, sir."

As Edwin puts his hand in mine to shake, I use my other hand to push Ryder's hand off my back. If he's upset about it, he doesn't show it.

"You are free to call me Edwin. Sir was my father," he says to me while still shaking my hand. Letting it go, he looks at Ryder before adding, "Rest his soul, but he was an awful man."

Ryder laughs with him at his statement, "I wouldn't say he was awful; he was just a businessman."

Edwin nods in agreement, "Too right you are, Ryder," he says before looking back to me, "Selena, how did you meet Ryder here?"

"Well, we met at my work and bonded over talking about business-like mind frames," I respond to him. Knowing this question would come up at a business gala, I decided to preplan a generic answer in advance.

Edwin seems to love my answer, his face showing more glee, "That sounds just like Ryder. Then the real question is: what do you think of this event so far?"

* * *

I see his question for what it is, a test. Next to me are two highly ranked people within this business and who possibly planned this event. This event is their territory, and I am only a guest. They were testing me as the new one to this group, seeing how honest I would be.

I take a deep breath before looking right into his eyes and responding, "What do I think so far? Seeing how I have been here less than an hour, I can't make a full assessment. But if I have to provide an answer, I would say that it is going well. There are more people in conversations than not and no one seems annoyed, so those conversations must be positive."

Edwin seems both pleasantly surprised and amused by my answer, "You certainly do have an eye for these things, don't you?"

"You asked what I thought. I am just responding with what I see since I don't have my own opinion," I answer him again before looking at Ryder, who is staring at me neutral faced. His laughter and joy from moments ago no longer showing.

"My girl, there is a difference between looking at what is going on and seeing," the older man says, complimenting me.

I don't answer him. Whatever test Edwin put in front of me, I'm guessing, is passed based on his response. Ryder appears to be listening and watching our interaction. For someone that was so excited for me to meet the people around him, he seems much less eager now.

Ryder puts his hand on Edwin's shoulder, grabbing his attention, "Edwin, you asked me a question in our previous conversation. I just remembered there is this business model that my father put together but never used. We can modify it now to have greater benefits. Would you take a second to look at it?"

Ryder is in the throws of showing his jealous side. It isn't just his envious side, but a fit of jealousy for his people's attention.

My mind for business and people prompted him to invite me tonight, but now it looks like he is threatened by it.

Edwin hesitates for a second before answering him, "Sure, Ryder, I don't mind."

As the two men walk off to look at whatever Ryder was talking about, I take the time to walk around—observing the crowds of people in small groups. Some of them stopping me to mention how lovely my dress is. I thank them and continue moving through the room, sipping on the contents of my glass.

"Good evening Madame." I turn to look at a lady to my right. She is wearing a black dress, simple jewelry, neat hair in a bun, and is middle-aged.

"Good evening. I'm sorry we haven't been introduced yet. I don't know your name."

"Abigale, darling," she responded, moving to stand in front of me.

"Pleasure to make your acquaintance. Selena Wilson." I responded, placing my hand out for her to shake. She takes my hand with a small smile.

"Pleasure is all mine. I am the one disrupting your thoughts currently. I saw you and realized you must be new to the group. I am the President of the Board; this is my house."

I look around at the architecture, "This house is breathtaking."

Abigale looks around with me, "Yes, it is. A family house passed down for generations." She replies matter-of-factly. There is no boasting or privileged tone. I gain the feeling of respect towards her. This crowd seems stuffy with privilege and ownership but not her. She states things how they are.

She turns her gaze back to me at this moment, "Did you come with anyone tonight?"

"Yes, with Ryder"

She nods her head slightly several times, registering my answer. Her face shows no emotion, but her eyes remained trained to my face, "I see. He is a pretty important person. That sounds like an interesting story there."

"There's not much to tell. Ryder and I have known each other for a short time. We share similar minds, so he invited me."

She stays contemplative for a moment, "I feel like you're the underdog that everyone underestimates and never sees coming."

I blink through my surprise at her statement. That is not how I saw this conversation going, especially at such a high-end party.

I said the only thing that I could think to say, "Thank you?"

Abigale gives me a small smile again, showing amusement in my response. She lightly touches my left shoulder and seems to talk more softly, "You will always find allies in the unlikeliest of places, Selena."

Abigale looks past me to a set of people coming down the stairs, "If you will excuse me, I need to see to some other guests, but I have no doubt we will speak again," she says, excusing herself.

I can briefly hear her say Henry as her voice floats back to me. I am trying to grasp the unusualness of the conversation we just had. To understand Abigale's vagueness or see through to the context that I was missing. No answers come to me.

I look at the drink still in my hand, mostly gone and most likely room temperature—I down the rest of what is in my glass right before Ryder walks up to me.

"There you are. I thought you left me already, and I was going to have to send out a search party."

"No, I didn't leave. I wanted to give you the space to have your conversation. I was just walking around, talking to people, and enjoying the building."

His eyes look at me pointedly, "Talking to people without me? About what?"

I squint my eyes at him, "Without you? You do realize I am a person that can function without you. In fact, I would have you know, I have been doing it my whole life."

Ryder responds quickly after realizing his miss-step, "It wasn't meant to sound that way."

I raise my hand up to stop him from continuing, "I think that is exactly what you meant to say, Ryder. I understand this is your scene, and these are your people. Is this not why you brought me along? To mingle with them?" I hand him the empty glass I'm holding onto tightly. "Now, if you will excuse me, I am going to walk around and do just that, mingle."

With that, I turn in the opposite direction I'm facing and start to walk away from him. I end up in a different section of the house that has a small balcony. Just outside the French doors sits two very well-groomed plants on either side. The plants are slightly taller than me and are light green, complementing the doors' color.

I look out over the railing at the beautiful garden resting on the side of the building. Magnolias and Rysk Blastjarnas are showing the beginning of their blooms. I look up, seeing the partially clouded sky obscuring the moon and stars. The moon is showing its resilience by shining even when trying to be tucked away. It seems the sky understands my mood more than this man.

• • •

Acceptance: The Beginning

At no point does Ryder chase after me, which is fine because, honestly, I don't want to see him right now. Why did I agree to come here tonight with him? Ryder is becoming more and more insufferable. He sure is acting more jealous than enthusiastic for someone who wanted me to hang out and be here tonight with him. I like his confidence, but it seems like he is trying to control me. The thought of someone trying to take something else from me after giving up so much already is insulting.

I'm stuck in my thoughts so much I don't notice when my fist slams down. A small outer edge of the railing chips off, bringing me out of my cloudy mind. I sigh with regret knowing full well this beautiful home belongs to Abigale. I change my focus to the night sky instead of my mistakes to stay out on the balcony a little longer, figuring out my actual reason for being invited and collecting my bearings.

Nearby inside the house, I hear voices that sounded slightly raised, coming off hurried and anxious. One sounded like a man, with the other a female.

Moving towards the doorway, I look around the area through the glass panes to see what is going on. To the right side were some sitting chairs, flowers, smaller architectural pillars, and two figures. One of those figures is Ryder on the side of one pillar, and the width of the column mostly concealed the female figure. The only thing I could see of her is a red dress and some of her back. Her hair is shoulder-length, blonde, layered with black highlights.

* * *

I see Ryder talking with his hands adamantly in a small area close to his chest. The female shakes her head at him. His face turns angry, pointing at her aggressively. I hear him say, "You need to step up," then it's too quiet to hear. She shakes her head again and turns to leave. Ryder quickly grabs her arm and pulls her back to him. He says something to her while appearing to have a death grip on her wrist. She pulls her arm away from him and slaps him across the face.

I'm watching the scene unfold, standing ready in case I need to jump in to help her. I have no idea how he would react if that happened. There is no way Ryder would act irrationally at such a nice work gala event, especially when most of the people he knew were in the same building. His cheek is slightly red as he turns his head back towards the female. I can hear him clear his throat and pointedly straighten his tux. He says something, then points to the side towards a door.

The female figure turns to leave, which is when I get to see the side of her face. Her features were graceful, even with her stern expression. She seems like she can handle herself if the occasion should arise. She walks smoothly to the door and disappears through it.

A man comes up to Ryder then and whispers in his ear. They leave the area hurriedly. This is the best moment to leave the balcony area without being spotted or considered suspicious. As casually as possible, I walk out of the balcony area. I think it is time for me to leave this ridiculous environment and go home. I head to the stairs, weaving around people.

● ● ●

I see Abigale talking to guests still but also drinking some of the champagne. She looks over to me as I'm about to reach the stairs and nods. I am not sure what the nodding is saying exactly, but I nod back. I start heading up the stairs. I reach the area where Ryder first found me at the beginning of the evening. I hear quick steps approaching me. I turn to see Ryder, and a sense of déjà vu comes to my mind. Unintentionally, I hold my breath waiting to see what he has to say.

Chapter: 12

"Where are you going? Are you leaving already?" he looks worried or anxious, which is surprising.

I look at him suspiciously when I reply, "I appreciate you inviting me tonight, Ryder. It has been a different experience. It is time for me to head home though."

"Why would you go home now? It has barely been half the evening," he asks, trying to counter my response.

"I don't want to be here any longer. I think I have made my mark on enough people tonight," I respond to him.

"No, you can't leave yet. I want to introduce you to some other people."

His statement makes me laugh, but not in a good way. This is his way of trying to convince me to stay with him. There is no asking, and this barely counts as persuasion. There's no benefit for me in staying; it's all in his favor. Usually, this is where I would think spending time with him was a positive thing. But with his behavior of abandoning me and bossing me around tonight, I now feel differently.

"I'm leaving Ryder. Thank you for your hospitality tonight. I'll talk to you later," I say with a bit of exhaustion in my voice. With that, I turn around and head out the front doors. I walk in my heels to the next metro station.

My journey home is quickly filling with thoughts of the evening. How dare Ryder try to change me, control me. My life has been fine this far without someone trying to get close to me and with minor casualties of feelings. My whole upbringing was about being taught control. Control for my emotions and actions. Ryder is pushing my boundaries too hard for what he wants, trying to get me to bend to him. Maybe he is so used to getting his way that he can't handle someone like me. I scuff at that thought; no one is like me.

When I left, the look he gave me was an expression of disappointment, and it's not familiar to me. Growing up, I always felt disappointed in myself, but rarely did I see it on the face of people around me. I'm not too fond of the feeling I keep getting from it. I reach my destination and feel some of the stress fall away. I'm ready to change out of these clothes.

I take the elevator to my apartment on the third floor. Even though I wasn't at the party for too long, it felt like I was there forever. Observing people can be exhausting. There were many new faces, people were acting weird, and figuring out what everyone was saying past their words took energy. I wish everyone would just say what they mean instead of making me guess. It's ridiculous sometimes.

Upon getting into the safety of my walls, I start taking my jewelry off. I feel pretty accomplished at playing with others in a social setting. I put my jewelry on my dining table. The next thing I need to shed is these shoes. My feet are really starting to hurt since my everyday footwear are boots. A sigh of relief leaves me as I remove the offending objects.

The outfit I decide to go with is yoga pants and a hoodie. I immediately hang up the dress. I may be sloppy sometimes, but not with something this exquisite. I stare at it for a second before putting it away, lightly running my hand over its blue color. I hope there will be another chance to wear this piece of clothing again. Perhaps with different shoes next time.

Heading to the bathroom to take apart the rest of my makeup and hair, I look at the clock. Regardless of the hour, I decided to head over to Uncle's shop to go to the training room by myself.

When I get to the shop, the lights are off, and everything looks peaceful. Uncle probably went to bed early. Retrieving the extra key he gave me, I let myself in. Locking the door again behind me, I make my way to the training room in the dark. I skip the regular meditating beforehand since it's just me in the room.

I start with some fluid motions combined with blocks, punches, and kicks. With each kick and punch, I let out my frustration. Frustration with the experience that happened tonight. Frustration with people being so mysterious. It's combined with the disappointment that this one person tried to take control of me and take my choices away by manipulation. My body seems to be moving faster through the stances with the increase of frustration I let surface.

Soon I am moving without thinking. My instincts seem to be taking over. I am in a dance with an invisible partner. An emotion is building up inside me that I do not fully understand. My ears start to hear muffled noises that sound like a consistence of someone speaking. No words can be identified clearly. Another voice in a different tone comes in just as muffled. I can't hear them but the more it goes on, the more it makes me angry. The muffled voices seem to start coming in more transparent and more urgent.

Then it comes in clear as day. A man's voice yelling,
"Stop!"

The yelling brought me back to my present state. My eyes refocus, my movements have ceased, and my breathing is erratic. My body has a top layer of sweat. Somehow, I'm both furious and sad at the same time. But it is not clear why or who it is meant for. Looking into the mirror, the brightest green I have ever seen is sitting in my reflection. There also seems to be tears coming down my face. I get out of my stance and reach my hand up to touch my tears.

What just happened?

* * *

I was training, zoned out, and heard people talking that weren't here. Among other things, I did not seem to be very much in control during it. My eyes being any indication, along with my other hand in a tight fist. I need to get this under control right now—breath in, breath out. Unclench your hands, I tell myself, just like you were trained to do your whole life. With each breath, I can feel my blood pumping loudly through my veins.

After several deep breaths, I get everything back to normal. I use my hoodie to wipe my tears off my face. Exhaustion is trying to creep into my being, and today has been a very eventful day. It's time to get home to bed, to sleep the stress away. As I exit the training room to lock up, Uncle comes through the other door from the apartment. Light streams in from behind him, illuminating the shop slightly.

"Leaving already? Did you want me to train with you?"

I shake my head as I turn off the lights to the training room, "No, I just wanted to do some solo training on form and fluidity. I am pretty tired, so I'm going to head home to bed."

"If that's what you want to do. Is there anything you want to talk about?"

Yes, I went to a social event I probably should have said no to, and I ended up in a trance-like state, hearing voices that don't exist. I just don't have the energy to get into it.

* * *

"No, not really. I just wanted to get some energy out," I give him a small smile and raise my hand in a wave, "I'll see you tomorrow, Uncle."

I walk to the front door, using my key to unlock and relock again as I leave. By the time I'm relocking the door to head home, Uncle is already back upstairs with his door shut. I never lied to him during that conversation; what I said was all true. I just did not want to talk about what happened tonight right now. Not with him or anyone. Sometimes the brain needs more time to process what is happening before addressing it with others.

Arriving at home a short time later, I immediately change into pajamas. My only goal in life right now, this very second, is going to sleep. Plopping down in bed, I toss the covers over me. By fate, my phone lights up in the darkened room. A groan leaves my mouth from the effort. I look at what lit up my screen at this time of the evening. It ends up being a text from Melanie.

Melanie: How was the night?

I throw a quick text together as a response.

Me: I'm exhausted and heading to bed. I'll tell you about it tomorrow.

After responding, the phone is put back to its place upside down on my side table. My eyes close to get the much-needed rest for my body, physically and mentally.

What seemed like seconds after falling asleep, a familiar scent comes to me. It is the kind of smell that no matter your mood, it calms you, like a fond memory of a holiday. This scent in particular, though, I have only known once before in a dream. This brought me to the realization that I was, in fact, dreaming. I tentatively reach out my hand and touch what appears to be the same soft skin as the last time.

For a couple of seconds, I let the relaxation settle in and allow the warmth of the situation to soothe me.

My curiosity wins shortly after that, as I continue to search for the answers to who this is and why it feels like they know me to a degree no one else does. I push my mind to talk with them or pull back to see the person's whole picture. Soon it is discovered that the more I push the limits, the more nothing happens. Frustration surges forward within me. I thought there would have been an adverse reaction to my frustration but instead, a warm blue light wraps around to comfort me.

I let the blue light soothe my irritation like aloe to a sunburn. It causes me to let go of the need for immediate resolution. I try a different approach. My mind reaches to caress the other spirit before me, spreading openness through my heart and soul. My reward for this action is a sweet smile, and I can't help but smile back. I have a little more freedom now, and the urge to keep touching them flies through me. My hand finds a comfortable spot just to the right of the smile that brings me happiness.

My mind snaps up and is met with the most beautiful eyes, a mix between gray and blue. They are full of so many different emotions, speaking volumes to me. This person is loving, confident, challenging, strong-willed, soulful, and powerful. These eyes in question also show a hint of mocking and mischief, resulting in a sly wink. My heart feels an involuntarily tug.

At that moment, my body decides to wake up. My eyes blink the sleep out of them. This time waking up is less confusing, even though I have as many questions as before. I'm feeling more at ease, with a glint of happiness dancing its way across my heart. Even though the mystery behind why this is happening is still there, it appears that I have little to no control over it. Which I'm okay with right now.

Whatever is going to happen, I have to accept it and try simultaneously to figure it out. That, however, would have to wait. My main concern right now is to meet up with Melanie and review what happened the night before.

Chapter: 13

I organize to meet Melanie for coffee that morning to give her the run-down she is craving on the Ryder situation and the night in general. But the unique dream I experienced had thrown off my morning routine, making me late to meet with her.

By the time I arrive at the meeting place, it's easily fifteen minutes past the scheduled time we agreed. Jogging across the street, I spot Melanie through the glass, sitting at a table.

I hurry inside to approach her. Melanie sees me as she is moving her cup of coffee to her mouth. One of her eyebrows raises in a statement over her cup. I smile apologetically at her and notice an extra cup of coffee at the empty seat.

"You ordered my coffee for me?" I ask as I sat down in the empty seat.

"Yes. Once I realized you were running late, I knew you would need it when you arrived, mainly because you are usually never this late for anything. You also get very cranky in the morning, especially when you are running late. Usually, you only order from two options, so I guessed." She answered with a nonjudgmental smile.

"You're a great friend," I say, letting out a breath before taking several drinks. The drink is spot on to what I would have ordered.

Melanie points at me, "Your best friend, in fact. So, what is making you so messy today?"

I don't answer right away, collecting my thoughts on what to say, "It was a weird night with Ryder, and then after I had odd dreams that just threw me off. I'm still adjusting."

"Want to tell me about it?" she asks me the question, but her eyes are telling me I don't have a choice.

I softly chuckle. Melanie is being polite about asking me when we both knew that if I said no as an answer, it would not have been dropped very quickly. So, I tell her the overview of it.

"I went to Ryder's event, as you know," She rolls her eyes and nods, "The people there weren't too bad. I had a lot of compliments on my outfit," that statement made her smile, "Ryder was acting hot and cold. Even with him inviting me to be there with him, he got jealous of my attention. He kept calling me dear, he didn't like that I talked to other people without him, and his attitude towards me seemed controlling and presumptuous. It didn't sit well with me, especially since we haven't spent a ton of time together. I left the party before it was over and told him that I would talk to him some other time."

She is drinking her coffee and listening carefully the entire time. When I finished talking, she scrunched up her nose, "He called you dear?" I nod in response, "That is a bit presumptuous. Then again, he invited you to a work party after a day of knowing you. He seems to move quickly." She pauses to think, then continued, "What happened after you left him there?"

My shoulders shrug as I'm looking into my half-empty coffee, "Nothing, I guess. I walked away from him and went home. No contact, no running after me, I just went home."

After I deliver my response, I raise my eyes to look at Melanie. Her face is showing contemplation.

"For someone who pushed so hard for you to meet up with them, only to let you walk away? Are you actually going to talk to him again after all this?" She asked.

Melanie is voicing all the thoughts and questions I have been battling in my head. She's just making me face the reality of it now, instead of being trapped in my mind to torture me later. I drink my coffee, thinking about what she is asking me before answering her.

"Truthfully, even if he did follow me while I was leaving, anything he would have said or did wouldn't have changed my mind. I saw who he is, and let me tell you, I'm not impressed.

He has a chance to redeem himself, but there isn't much room left in my patience for him. Ryder puts forth effort, and then it runs out halfway through because things don't go his way."

A comfortable silence falls between us as Melanie registers what I have said to her. My words are painting her a picture to envision. She is excited I am getting out there but concerned about me getting hurt.

After some time, Melanie responds, "Selena, if you do or don't want to give him another chance, that is up to you. But I want to remind you that there are more people out there too. Now, I want to know about these weird dreams you had?"

My thoughts immediately flash to the blue eyes I saw and feel the tug inside of me, "I don't remember them very well. It just gave me feelings of being out of control."

She starts to fidget with her empty cup, "Yeah, that would put you out of sorts today. You don't like being out of control. The dream sounds like a metaphor for the experience you had with Ryder. I read somewhere that dreams can mirror experiences and feelings from the day."

"Maybe," I respond, thinking about her attempt at explaining my problems. In this area, she didn't have all the information. Like that these dreams have been going on longer than she thinks, involving a person I don't know.

"What are you going to do today?" Melanie pushes on.

"I work tonight, but I thought about going out on Tuesday to Revolution. To let out some of my stress."

Melanie smirks, she knows that when I go to Revolution, it usually means I want to be alone. And by alone, that means alone with other people showing me affection, "I'm working that night. So try not to get into trouble because I won't be able to bail you out."

"I'll do my best to keep myself out of any sticky situations," I respond and roll my eyes at the same time. That happened one time, and it seemed like I couldn't live it down since then. I picked up a girl who was already in a relationship—finding out only when we were drunkenly getting a cab to my place, and her partner came running after us out of the club.

I look at the clock; the time is getting late. I needed to start the rest of my day before work. We finish up our visit and part ways. With such an unusual several days, I'm excited to get back out to the club on Tuesday. Back to something I'm familiar with. I count down the days and hours.

The rest of Sunday and Monday seem to pass quickly, with work as a distraction. Tuesday morning finally comes, and with it, my excitement. I used to go to Revolution about once a month, sometimes several times, depending on my stress level. This club is a place that I can be who I want and feel free. Melanie would, on occasion, come with me. Only when she needed to let go too. Most of the time, she knew I needed this outlet and wouldn't come. A place I can go to with no responsibility.

* * *

Recently I hadn't been going because of all of the happenings and events. Is it possible to have withdrawals from a building? Maybe it isn't the building but the people and the experience. Since frequenting less, I feel a bit edgier, which may have played a part in several poor decisions I have made recently.

All of that is going to change today.

The day is mine to spend; however I want. Waffles for brunch, catching up on some shows, and taking the time to figure out what I want to wear tonight. I feel relatively carefree even after leaving Ryder behind three days ago. He hasn't tried to reach out these past several days. After talking with Melanie that Sunday morning, I don't overthink the situation. If he wants to speak to me, he will, and if he doesn't, then I won't cry about it. Instead, I'm listening to some music, singing along, and slowly getting ready to go out.

While going through my make up to feel out what I wanted to do, my phone starts to ring. Without thinking about it, I reach for it and answer with a hello. On the other side of the line, I hear a deep voice answer my greeting.

"Hey Selena, it's Ryder. I know we haven't talked in a couple of days. I wanted to check on you."

I stop going through my make up when I hear his voice. "Hey, Ryder. I've been a bit busy, but I am doing okay."

"I am glad. Edwin was asking about you after you left. I told him you had a long day," I roll my eyes not responding to him. If he wants to talk to me, he needs to work for it, "I wanted to see if you were up to meeting me tonight."

I answer honestly, resuming what I'm doing before Ryder called, "I already have plans tonight. I'm in the process of getting ready now." Pausing, I think back to Melanie's question about giving him another chance, "Do you want to come with me?"

"Maybe, where are you going?" he asks before answering fully.

"I'm heading to the club Revolution."

He answers faster than I thought he would have, considering our now developing past.

"I don't like going to dance clubs. They are for a different type of crowd than me. We can meet up on a different day."

His statement causes me to stop what I'm doing again; anger flares up in me. Did he just say he's too good to go? My brain is having difficulty understanding how he is taking something I enjoy and turning it into a negative, especially when he contacted me to hang out.

I'm quiet. The length of time is long enough that it causes Ryder to check if I'm still on the line. "Selena? Are you still there? Did I lose you?" Did you lose me, indeed?

I clear my throat to respond, "Yes, Ryder, I am here. Sorry, I was preoccupied for a moment," I can hear him huff for a second when I say that, "Out of curiosity, you said you didn't like dance clubs, that they weren't your scene for fun. You come to the bar to drink. How is the dance club different than that?"

When Ryder answers, I can hear the undertone of agitation in his voice, "The bar is where you can go to talk and drink with music in the background. A club is loud with music and people that do whatever they want. They are out of control and disruptive."

I can't help what comes from me next, "Out of control and disruptive? Wow, Ryder. That perspective seems a bit harsh, especially since I am grouped in that category. I would, in reality, call it liberating and freeing."

"I'm not calling you specifically disruptive. If that were true, I wouldn't be trying to see you at all," Ryder responds. I can hear his tension rise with mine. It's all starting to feel like a lover's quarrel without the love.

"Then why did you ever ask me to meet up with you? Why did you give me your number? Please enlighten me, Ryder, because all I see right now is that I don't act how you want me to." I rush out of my mouth, gripping hard to the phone and counter. This man is infuriating! Who does he think he is?

I feel my anger pulsing through me as everything comes to the surface involving this one person. I hear a sharp cracking noise around me. I look at the spot where my hand is located and see a break in the countertop. There goes some of my deposit on the apartment. My eyes are starting to glow green in the mirror from my temper. This situation briefly reminds me of the balcony incident from the night of the gala. I'm taking this as another sign that Ryder is nothing good for me. I take several quiet deep breaths to calm down.

Ryder doesn't seem to notice anything that is happening on my end. It is doubtful he can hear over the music and takes a second to answer my interrogation. I'm not sure if he is thinking of an answer, trying to keep his temper under control, or surprised into silence at the turn in the conversation. Either way, I'm grateful for the break away from accusing tones on what is supposed to be a fun and carefree day.

When Ryder finally does answer, his voice is even, void of any agitation or anger previously present.

"I gave you my number because I saw something in you that reminded me of myself."

A sigh leaves me. I get what he is saying. I saw it too, which is why I called him at all. But I see it less and less now. Another deep breath leaves me, leveling my emotions.

I match his tone of voice when responding, "I hear you, Ryder, but fundamentally we are very different. These kinds of conversations are extremely unhealthy, and I don't want to be around you if this is how it's going to be. I'm going to get off the phone and get ready for the plans I made without you. Have a good night."

• • •

As I move the phone away from my ear to hang up, I can hear him say my name through the earpiece. Without giving him another thought, I hang up. Taking a deep breath, I look at my reflection in the mirror, letting go of the heavyweight that Ryder created.

My eyes go back to my makeup in front of me. Its presence is reminding me that my task is uncompleted, music still playing in the background. I put on an energizing song to get me back into my space. Leaving all the heavy emotions behind me, I start singing along, picking up my concealer.

Chapter: 14

In bright red letters sits the Revolution sign. As the sign grows larger, so does my excitement for the evening of possibilities. I can feel the bass from the music softly caressing my ears. I pull open the factory-made door and let the music fill my mind.

Approaching the admissions area with the bouncer next to it, I see it is Gar.

His face lights up when he sees me coming, "Hey Selena! I haven't seen you in a while. How have you been? We were missing you."

I wink at him; he was always sort of cute in his bubbly, happy kind of way, "Hey Gar, I think what you truly missed was someone babying you." This produced a laugh from both of us because of the truth of it. When I used to come here, I would check on him to give him some company if it was slow every couple of hours. He wouldn't stay in the admissions area the whole time, but it got redundant staying in the same small space for a long time.

I lay down the money for entering and give him a brief explanation, "I just took a short vacation, but I am back now, so don't worry. How is your boyfriend?"

He smiles at me, handing over the change, "Leon is doing great. He started a new job, we're doing great, and I don't know how I'm so lucky to have found him. By the way, a girl was asking about you. She will be happy to see that you came in tonight."

I raise my eyebrows slightly. I didn't have many friends, but I did use to dance with many people while here. I know some of the people in the crowd but mainly come here to dance my pain and stress away. Whenever people talk to me, I speak to them but never give them any personal information about myself. Unless of course, I take them home with me. Regardless, I always feel like I can be whoever I want to be here.

I look at him sideways before responding, "Gar, do you have more information about this female you are speaking of? Or are you going to leave me in suspense?"

Gar laughs at his own mischievous behavior, "Well firstly, I missed you, so I'm people. Also, a woman was asking about you coming in a couple of times this past weekend. Although she did not know your name specifically, her description of who she was looking for only really fit you. There is only one of you, after all."

A confident smile lands on my face, "Don't I know that!"

Gar lightly laughs at my confidence, "Have fun tonight. Stay out of trouble!"

Moving towards the inner doors, I yell back to him over my shoulder, "That happened one time!"

I hear a hearty laugh from his direction, "One time is enough for me!"

I walk through the inner door to the main club. The music is surrounding my entire body, and the bass bounces off me like my own heartbeat. The inside looks like a modernized warehouse with go-go girls on blocks wearing neon green and pink fishnet shirts and yarn dreads to match.

My outfit is pretty simple, black pants with an electric blue design on the side and a black tank top. I walk to the bar and order a vodka shot to jump start on the mood—the club goers dancing in a mass to my left. Around me, three others are drinking their choice of poison. Everyone else is on the floor. With the boost of confidence now running through my stomach, I relocate to the dance floor for some fun.

After a half-hour of dancing, I am starting to feel more like myself. I lift my hands above my head and dance by myself. I'm letting all the previous weights lift off my soul. Soon, though, I will have to stop for water. As the song ends, I feel a mental tug causing me to look around. Everyone I can see is laughing, drinking, or dancing. It feels like someone is staring at me somewhere within the room. I sway my way over to a water bottle at the bar and pay. But the feeling of another person's eyes on me is still there. I pack away half the bottle in one gulp and visually search around the room. No one can be seen giving me their full attention at that moment.

After finishing the water off, I quickly chase it with a shot. Easily pushing it down my throat, I find my way back to the dance floor. If someone is watching, I can see them easier on the floor. Doing this will give me a better view of the entire room.

There is a brown-haired girl near the middle of the group of dancers, motioning me over to her. I put on a smile and make my way over to her. Upon reaching her vicinity, she takes my hand and starts to dance against me. Matching her dancing, we fall into a rhythm. I feel the soft mental tug again like before. This is not the person whose eyes I felt watching me, but it's a nice distraction right now.

She moves her head closer to my ear and yells over the music, "My name is Gina."

"Selena," I respond.

She smiles at me, "I come here all the time but never dared to approach you before. I am glad you started to come back."

I give my half-smile, "I was on sabbatical, but that is over with." It sounds like this is the person that Gar mentioned.

Gina pulls me closer to her as the next song comes on. Two songs later, my eyes lift to see a woman staring at me. Even though there are countless people between us, it feels like there's none. She is leaning against the side wall just off the dance floor. The woman has blonde hair with black highlights. This is a face I already know from the work party that Ryder invited me to. Is she following me?

I break away from my dance partner, thanking Gina. I move around several people and couples to get to her. She has on black jeans and a sexy red top. Her arms are across her chest, and her left shoulder is holding all her weight against the wall. Right before reaching her, she pushes off the solid mass and moves away from me giving me her back. After several steps, she looks behind at me to make sure I'm following, then smiles. She is moving us away from the music to a quieter area. She stops off to the side of the hallway to the bathrooms, turning around to face me. I smile a cautious smile.

"Hi," she says. It may have come across as casual, but she is the one driving this situation right now.

"Hey," I respond with equal calmness. She doesn't say anything right away. I continue the conversation feeling a need to fill the growing void, "My name is Selena."

She smiles wider, complementing her beautiful features, "I'm Skylar."

"I saw you at that work party a couple of days ago."

Her smile falls slightly. She evidently didn't see me during that time. She shrugs one shoulder nonchalantly, trying to act coy, "I didn't stay very long. It isn't my preferred scene."

I look at her with more focus, digging for information, "You were dressed like it's your scene. If you didn't want to be there, then why were you?"

She scuffs unintentionally, it seems almost as if the idea is ridiculous, "I shouldn't have even been there at all, but I am friends with one of the families. They invited me. Telling them "no" wasn't an option. So, I showed up to make an appearance, then left when I could."

I nod at her response, not finding any immediate holes in it. For the time being, I am keeping the knowledge to myself that she not only knows Ryder but was arguing with him. I reach out my hand for her to shake, "Nice to meet you, Skylar."

She extends her hand to put into mine. When our hands touch, I feel an exchange of energy. It isn't a feeling of energy like physical electricity but of knowing. It's a shock of understanding. The second it happens, recognition floods my mind. All the unsureness is no longer there. I know all the dreams belong to this one person, but it's like I already knew her. How can someone have so much control over a person without ever knowing them before? And yet, here she is in front of me.

Any doubt leaves whenever I look into her eyes, and she touches my arm. I know these eyes better than any other person. My mind flashes back to the dream a couple of nights before, seeing these beautiful, telling eyes.

Her current facial expression is of concern, but her eyes say she understands, "Are you okay? The look you are giving me is weird."

I'm facing a situation I have never dealt with before. Being close to others is something I am not familiar with. Opening up to emotions that I'm trained to keep closed for the safety of myself and others is something I'm not familiar with. How does one reverse this and still keep everything sacred?

"I'm not sure of how to answer that question right now. Let me get back to you on that," I answer Skylar, trying to cope with what is happening.

She smiles an almost knowing smile. Oh yea, she is good, like a pro. I will have to tread very, very lightly with this one, especially after what happened with Ryder. This isn't going to be very easy for me.

Skylar removes her hand from my arm. The absence generates a feeling of wanting to reach out, to touch her.

"Is that how you get all the girls? Telling them they cause you to be speechless?"

"It's not that I'm speechless. It is just that this is a unique meeting."

A sweet smile is written across her mouth, "If you say so. Well, I need to get going. I guess I will see you around here." She says it so offhandedly. Then Skylar casually turns away from me to leave.

● ● ●

I immediately grab her arm to pull her back to me, which causes her to be closer than she was the first time. I quickly let go of her arm, "You stared me down on the dance floor, lured me away to talk, and now you are leaving? Can I at least have your number?"

A look of surprise flashes on Skylar's face from the movement. But as she listens to my small rant, a playful smile is developing on her face. She reaches in her pocket and gett out a folded piece of paper, "Oh right, that's what I forgot to do. Give you my number." She winks at me and puts it in my hand.

With the paper in my hand, I stare at her in disbelief. She had her number written out on a piece of paper before I even saw her tonight. Her goal, her intent, was to give me her number the entire time. But only if I asked for it.

"Call or text me." She turns to leave again, delicately moving her fingers in the air in a little wave.

I shake my head and softly laugh, putting the paper in my pocket. Of course, I will.

I shout after her, "I'll think about it."

This statement causes her to glance back at me, with her smirk still in place, before disappearing through the doors to exit.

Chapter: 15

The next morning comes in a blur. Literally, not metaphorically, a blur. Last night after Skylar and I met, I went back to grab a couple more drinks to keep from calling her until today. Concentrating on drinking and dancing provided the distraction I needed. Any self-control in this situation was needed— in the form of not contacting Skylar the second she left. After distracting myself for some time, I managed to get home to bed. By the time I woke up, my mind still seemed to be a bit groggy with blurred vision. Nothing a shower and a pancake breakfast couldn't fix.

Once I feel more rejuvenated with the afternoon quickly approaching, I locate the paper with Skylar's number on it to put into my phone. Then I sit there with my phone in my hands; a blank screen is staring at me.

What does one say to the woman that they see in their dreams? Without seeming creepy. Am I overthinking this? Yes, absolutely. Will she care what I actually message her?

No, probably not. I settle on a simple straightforward message.

Me: Morning Skylar, it's Selena

I turn the ringer up on my phone and lay it down on the table. I walk away to work on my hair. In the end, I decided to go with a straightened style. By the time my hair is half straightened and half wavy, my phone goes off. I look at myself in the mirror. My hands are on the equipment, running down a strand of hair. Whatever just came through can wait until I am finished with the other half of my hair.

Then another sound comes through, indicating another message. My hands pause as I take a deep breath to curve any building excitement. I focus on my current task. When I feel comfortable enough with my hair's style, the machine is turned off and unplugged.

Skylar: Morning Selena, it is nice to hear from you finally.

Skylar: I thought you would have contacted me sooner than this, in truth.

She is openly admitting that she was waiting for me to reach out to her. That is bold. I'm not sure how I want to respond, so the truth is the best bet.

Me: I wanted to wait until today to contact you with more clarity and a sound mind.

Skylar: Which is surprising considering you were the one who asked for my number.

Me: Says the girl who had the number already written out in her pocket before I asked.

There is a pause in the exchange as she deals with the honest facts I just handed to her. She set the tone for an open conversation. Who am I not to deliver.

Skylar: lol Touche.

Skylar: I couldn't pass up the chance that I wasn't prepared.

Me: Do you usually walk around random places with your number already written down to hand out to people?

Skylar: No, but I had a feeling that last night was going to be different.

Skylar: Are you available to hang out this afternoon?

Me: I won't be able to. I have to work tonight and will need to be getting ready soon to go in.

Skylar: Okay, fair. It's not truly a rejection, just a delay in timing. Where do you work?

Me: I work at a bar as a bartender.

Skylar: Does this bar have a name?

Me: Yes.

Skylar:…Are you going to tell me what it is?

Me: No. If you want to know where I work, you will need to find me. ;)

Skylar: Okay. I like the challenge. I will see you later tonight.

After our conversation, I slowly start to get ready for work, allowing the time to shake off any morning remnants. Today, getting prepared for work is done with extra care, knowing Skylar's full intention to find me and show up. When I go to work, I always dress to impress. Just on slower days, like tonight, I usually did not put as much effort into it as Fridays.

Even though I just met Skylar, the connection felt physically tangible. With my training in self-preservation and control, Skylar's presence makes me feel very not in control. Whenever I think about the dreams and the first time I saw her, I feel less in control of our interactions. Putting my finishing touches on, I leave the house to head to work.

Once my shift starts, I forget about Skylar possibly showing up to visit me. I'm concentrating on what I need to get done. It's also a plus in the sense that if she ends up not coming in, there will be no immediate disappointment. Being entirely concentrated on work means roughly halfway through my shift, I'm in my zone and making sure customers leave the bar with a smile. I just finish up a refill and joking around with a patron when I hear someone slapping the bar top with their open palm.

"Excuse me! Bar hop, I need some assistance."

I quickly turn my head to see who just called me "bar hop".

My eyes immediately meet with Skylar's beautiful face. My face turns from confused to an amused smile in one breath.

● ● ●

Skylar is wearing dark blue jeans with a styled dark gray top. Her hair is wavy, and she is showcasing a simple black choker necklace with a matching bracelet. I walk as calmly as possible over to her and lean on the counter.

"Good evening, miss. I hear you need assistance with something."

She smiles wide and seems extremely pleased I'm playing along, "Yes, I sure do. I am in current need of refreshment. Do you know how many bars there are in this town?"

I give her a small laugh, "A lot."

She nods, "A lot. In fact, I went to at least four before finding you here."

Her statement makes me laugh harder, "How many drinks did you have before getting here?"

"Three."

"Alright, not as bad as I thought you would have said. What refreshment can I get you from this bar?"

She answers without pause, "Vodka Cranberry." She tilts her head, "Please."

"Coming right up." I push off the counter to move around to put her drink together. She says she went to four bars to find me. There is no real way to know if that is true. I want to believe her. The only thing to go off of is her word. As I'm thinking about her arrival, I can feel her eyes on me. I can't bring myself to look over at her. When I put her drink down, our hands meet. That feeling of knowing returns with it. We both connect to each other's eyes at the same time. Both of us at a standstill, neither one of us willing to make a move away. I want to ask her: Why is this only with her? What did it mean? It makes my heart feel pulled to her. The more I push the feeling down, the more it seems to pull at me. It feels beautiful and painful at the same time.

I pull my hand away first. Putting on my best smile to hide how I'm feeling, I address Skylar, "Since I caused you such difficulty finding me, the least I can do is buy this drink for you."

At that moment, more customers approach the counter. I give her a half-smile, then walked away. I move through the small burst of business while randomly looking over in her direction as discreetly as possible. Skylar remains at the counter where she is. She drinks some of the beverage through the straw. Then she stirs it a bit, with a small smile on her lips as she looks into the glass. Seeing her small smile causes me to smile.

Time moves quickly while I work, with twenty more minutes passing before I get a chance to go back to her. Skylar is patiently waiting with her empty glass, "You don't have to stay up at the counter the whole time, you know, right?"

Skylar pushes her glass forward to me and looks me over, "And give up the best seat in the house? I wouldn't dream of it." This isn't the first time someone has checked me out. It is just the first time that Skylar has openly checked me out. I feel my cheeks heat up slightly even as my willfulness tries to stop it. If Skylar notices, she doesn't let on.

"Did you want anything else to drink?" I ask while taking her glass to put in the dish container.

"A bottle of beer. I'll pay for this one, though."

"Sure, any certain kind?"

She leans forward and whispers, "Surprise me."

I wink at her and go hunt down a beer that I think represents her. We don't have a ton of selection available. I choose the best I can, feeling like a regular beer won't fit this extraordinary person. In this case, it ends up being a lighter beer with a twist of orange to it. It's a seasonal option we just got in.

I take off the top, putting it in front of her. "Here you go."

Skylar picks it up, looking at the label. She shrugs her shoulders and takes a drink, "I like it. It's light, breezy almost, with a kick of citrus." She looks at me with all seriousness, "Are you calling me sassy with the citrus?"

"Yes, yes I am."

She takes another sip looking at me over the bottle, "Yeah, that's fair."

The rest of the night continues with Skylar hanging out with me at the counter. She ends up getting a second bottle of the same beer. A couple of hours go by, with me helping customers who come up, completing my duties, and talking to her as I work. The conversations are random with an air of flirty undertones. Things are winding down, and it comes time for her to leave.

"I think it is time for me to close out my tab and head home," Skylar says with a bit of tiredness in her voice, handing me her card. I don't blame her for being tired. Considering she traveled around the city to find me.

"Sure. We close soon, anyway." I respond as I run her card. I hand her the paper to sign to finish up. As she is signing her name, I chime in, "Thank you for coming to visit me tonight."

Skylar's face livens up a bit from that statement, "Of course. I wanted to see you."

I'm slightly taken aback by her honest statement. She did also have several drinks before saying it, though.

Skylar grabs something from her pocket, folding it a couple of times in her hands.

She leans over the counter, putting her hand out, "This is for you."

I lean forward to reach what she is trying to give me. As soon as I lean forward, Skylar grabs the front of my shirt to pull me to her. She puts her other hand on my jawline. With her hand on my face, she moves my face to the side to kiss my cheek. I feel my face go bright red. Her actions completely catch me off guard, but I in no way want her to stop.

Skylar removes herself from my space and winks at me, "Don't forget to text me." Her body sways its way to the door. My eyes can't help watching her retreating figure. There are not many people who can make me feel like I have no confidence or finesse. After these two interactions, it is clear that she goes for what she wants. She is forward about it, and when she gets it, she usually makes it feel like it's your idea. She is a force to be reckoned with, and I'm getting addicted.

Chapter: 16

The next couple of weeks, I start picking up some extra shifts at the bar. Picking up these shifts makes it harder for Skylar and me to get together outside of her visiting me at work and text messages back and forth. Temporarily, we fall into a pattern of texting in the morning and afternoon. Then at night when I work, she will come to visit me, buying a drink or two. We chat about our favorite things and tell stories. However, Skylar does most of the talking when it comes to her favorite things. I turn the attention away from me as much as possible. Either from a lack of experiences or trying to keep some distance between us remains to be seen.

Skylar, at this moment, is doubling over in laughter on the counter. I am leaning in, listening to her every word. There is a smile showing ear to ear on my lips from how much she enjoys telling this story.

She wipes a tear away from her eye from all the laughing, "And then……and then my mom walks in. She stops midstride and just stands there. She doesn't say anything at all, just looks at me. I didn't know what to say to her. There were no words. So, I turned and ran as fast as I could. That is how I lost my freedom for three months."

I can't stop the laugh that comes out of me from her story. It's a story of young, reckless behavior and consequence. Even though the situation surrounding the story was a severe lapse of judgment, she told it with such passion and humor that anyone would laugh.

Skylar finishes her drink. Then turns her beautiful blue eyes to me, shining from her smile, "What about you? Do you have any crazy and ridiculous stories about being grounded?"

I chuckle at her description, "No, I can't say I have any crazy stories about being grounded."

She seemed surprised by my answer, "No? You seem like such a rebel like you would have a great story to tell."

I shrug my shoulders, smiling at her, "I'm afraid no such luck."

She tilts her head, "Huh, I did not expect that. What about your parents? What kind of people are they, besides the not grounding kind? Are they as cool as you?"

My smile falls, "My Uncle raised me. It's just the two of us."

Her eyes turn a shade sadder, "I'm sorry. We don't have to talk about it if you don't want to."

I straighten myself off the counter, grabbing her glass, "It is something I don't normally talk about, but I need to start getting ready to close. I should get back to it."

Skylar is still smiling, but it doesn't seem to reach her eyes like before, "I should head out anyways."

She hovers in a movement that is somewhere between wanting to say something and leaving. I don't walk away immediately to see what she does. Skylar reaches over to put several strands of my wavy hair behind my ear.

Somehow this action seems more intimate than her kissing me on the cheek the first night she visited. She looks at me like she is deep in thought and processing something—her hand now resting on the side of my face. I am studying her, trying to guess what is playing through her mind, to see what she feels. Something pulls her out of her thoughts. She smiles, taking her hand away from me. My instinct kicks in, making me want to follow her hand. I can't seem to help the slight lean towards her, trailing after her energy. Somehow, I stop myself and remain steady, managing to smile at her.

She winks at me, "Talk to you later." Just like all the other nights, my eyes watch her sway away from me towards the door.

Skylar leaving gives me enough visual observation to notice Melanie approaching me several feet away.

I give her a half-smile, putting Skylar's glass where it belongs, then returning to Melanie at the counter.

Melanie has a smile playing on her lips. She is trying to be stern but is having a hard time doing it, "I was going to ask why I haven't heard from you recently," she looks at the door that Skylar just left through, "but I see the reason why just left."

There is nothing I can do to prevent a small blush from rising on my face from embarrassment, "I talked to you yesterday. I told you I'm picking up extra shifts at work. What are you talking about, "I haven't heard from you recently"?"

Melanie fakes her feelings being hurt by holding her hand over her heart and exaggeratingly gasps, "I texted you earlier in the night, and there was never a response. You usually text me when you work but haven't lately. So, I came over to see why. I have no idea what happened since the club."

I shrug my shoulders, "I've been busy."

She smirks at me, throwing her thumb in the direction of the door, "Yeah, I saw that. What's going on? What's her name?"

I sigh, looking down the bar counter at the tasks I still need to complete, "I gave Ryder another chance. He blew it, so that's over. I ended up meeting her at the club when I went. Her name is Skylar."

Melanie raised her eyebrows, "The time you went to the club a couple of weeks ago? How many times has she come to visit you while you were working?"

I look her dead in the eyes, "Every night that I have worked since then. She has come in to order a drink or two and talk with me."

Melanie has a look of surprise written all over her face from my answer, "Wow, Selena. She comes in to get a drink, talks, and then what? Leaves to go home?" I nod my head, "I have never heard you say anyone has done that before in all the time you have worked here. She must like you."

I hear Joe's voice from the backroom, "Selena, can you come to the back? I need help with something."

"I have to go," I tell her as I move in Joe's direction.

Melanie raises her hands in defeat, "Alright, alright. Text or call me later so we can talk about this more, you hussy."

I don't even deem that with a verbal response but give her a patronizing smile and thumbs up.

By the time I get home, the feeling of exhaustion is more potent than any other work night this week. My mind seems cloudy. Skylar can't seem to stop running across my thoughts. I dream about her, I talk to her almost every day, and she visits me at work. She is everywhere. My urge to be close to Skylar multiplying with each conversation. I want her attention. It's making me feel vulnerable, and it scares me. Not a single person should control another with just a smile. Even with all of my training to handle my emotions and keep them in check, this seems uncontrollable. I try to push her out of my mind, even as these feelings seem to overtake my senses. It doesn't seem to work very well. At best, I can get these feelings to turn into a dull ache.

The only thing left to do at this point is to get ready for bed while I process the day. My fingers go to my messages on my phone, immediately hovering over Skylar's name. After weighing my options and considering my growing connection to Skylar, I decide to select Melanie's name instead.

Me: Hey

Melanie: Evening, miss popular

Me: eye roll emoji

Melanie: lol jk. So tell me about this girl Skylar?

Me: I know it is just her and her mom. She tells me some stories of them growing up. She is part of the HR team at her company.

Me: She is just a girl who has a great personality, is interested in what I have to say, and isn't pushy.

Melanie: OMG you really, really like her! Listen to you hahaha.

Melanie: Have you gone out on a date yet??

Me: No

Melanie: Slow and steady… nice! After your first real date, I want to meet her.

Me: We'll see what happens.

Melanie: Yea OKAY, "we'll see what happens" give me a break. At this rate, as long as she isn't a psychopath, you will probably be living with her in a couple of years.

Me: Night Melanie

Melanie: Niiiiggghhhttt

After ending the conversation with Melanie, my phone goes on the charger in its usual spot on my nightstand. I take a deep breath. Sometimes Melanie is helpful and not at the same time. She doesn't understand what I'm going through entirely. I'm not in a great position to explain it to her. The only solution I have left for me tonight is sleep. When I get comfortable, I drift off quickly.

Chapter: 17

While I am asleep, I feel stuck in a dream. Like literally, I'm stuck in a dream and can't get out or wake up. It is dark as night, and there are warped city buildings around me. Some buildings have a tinge of red or purple but not resembling anything in ordinary reality. I'm aimlessly walking around the streets in search of something. Something I can't remember but feels like it belongs to me. My mind feels fuzzy from wanting to solve a problem I can't see clearly. I know the solution, but my mind can't seem to form it into existence. The longer the feeling of inactivity and feeling of stuck continues, the more panicked I feel.

Shadows of what looks like people randomly start showing up on the distorted buildings. I see them at first, but when I look again to see who they are, they are gone. The shadows appear at a slow pace but gain momentum the longer I roam the streets. It gives the feeling of being chased, closed in on, or trapped. The dream seems to be turning into a nightmare quickly.

As I turn the corner in my nightmare street, there stands a door to what looks like a wooden cabin. It's very out of place with everything else around me. I jog to it and open the door to step in.

When the door closes behind me, there is a single room in my vision. The room has a fire lit in a fireplace. There are no other windows or doors. All previous weird happenings with warped shadow people and buildings are gone. I feel her presence arrive behind me but don't hear the door. It's like she just appears out of nowhere. She moves next to me, running her hand down my arm taking ahold of my left hand in hers. I feel our connection lightly pulsing.

I turn my head to her. She is already looking at me and says, "You are safe here."

I nodded still looking at her, "Why is this dream different than the others?"

Skylar's eyes turn mischievous, "I think it's because you are already dreaming in this one. Or it's because you were having a nightmare and needed something different."

I just look at her, not actually caring what answer she gives me. I'm happy to be in a different dreamscape with her.

I ask the question that I always wondered but never could ask before, "Is this normal for you? To have dreams with other people like this?"

* * *

Skylar answers me in a soft voice that can barely be heard, "No, this isn't a normal thing. These dreams have only happened with you."

She then moves in front of me, standing between me and the fireplace. Her voice once again fills with confidence, switching topics, "You never texted."

The feeling of dull agitation goes through me when she says it. The idea that I can't have an independent life away from her flaring up. Then I quickly realized the agitation is because I thought about it before going to sleep but decided not to contact her. I shake my head, feeling the fear of being open, vulnerable, and having to rely on someone to feel whole. The feelings are not only coming from that, but her calling me out on the inaction.

I stare at the reflection of the burning fireplace on the walls and respond, "I was busy."

She grabs my chin to make me look at her, "You can't hide your emotions here. Our connection is already there; we can feel each other's feelings. It's a dream. You can think what you want." Her hand goes back to the spot on my cheek where it was earlier. Running her fingers softly across my face, to my hairline, and down my neck slightly. "Do what we want."

Of course, she is right. I recognize that even if we don't understand why this is happening, she has a better grasp of the connection. After all, she runs all of the dreams and conversations and has been from the start.

Her hand on my skin tells me that she wants me to be closer to her. I'm staring at her lips. Skylar takes her thumb from the other hand running it across my bottom lip. Our eyes meet again, locking into this moment. Mirroring several different situations we've been in together before.

She asks again, "Why didn't you text me?"

Skylar may feel what I feel, but she can't understand my reasons for my choices. Panic rises in me as I answer honestly, "Being close to you scares me."

Skylar smiles. It's not a smile that's a mask, forced, or fake. It is a real genuine smile, "They are just conversations, Selena, nothing more."

I grab onto her arm still on my neck and squeeze it as I try to keep the panic and aching of being close to her down, "You and I both know that isn't true. I don't want to rely on you every day to be the thing to make or break me. A tone of voice or certain things that are said should not affect my entire mood. I should be strong without you."

Her arm and hand tense, reacting in a visceral way to this very earnest conversation involving real emotions and truths very quickly. Neither one of us expected any of this to happen, but here we are—no place to go except forward through it.

Skylar's face saddens slightly, "What I say and do shouldn't affect your day? Similar to when you don't text me at night when you usually do because that is what we are used to doing now?"

The feeling of fear of vulnerability intensifies. Skylar feels the exact same way; she is trying her best to protect herself too. "I…yes." I smile, softening my features to her, feeling genuine affection towards her, "Like that."

The muscles in her arm are pulling me forward. Her other hand is on the other side of my face. Skylar's lips are touching mine in an intimate private embrace, but it feels almost like a ghost touch. Light, airy, barely there. The emotions that are pushing me closer to her are less with so much of her skin touching mine. My hand is in her hair. I feel her essence, her being, all over me. It is reassuring me, guiding me, urging me. I feel her everywhere, but somehow, she is still only in front of me.

I wake suddenly in a somewhat confused state. I'm confused about why I'm in a different room and by myself. My heart seems to be racing, and my skin is on fire. As I sit up to get my bearings, the sheet moves down my arms and chest to my torso. The top of my skin seems to be sensitive to everything. Sensitive to my movements, the air, the sheets I'm on. It all has created a ghost memory of a feeling. An interaction that was not precisely physical but corporal enough to have left a hint of what can be. It's a whisper of what the future can hold if I move forward down that path.

I put my head in my hands to redirect my senses to something more in reality. The action does what I need it to do, calming the ghostly touches. What it also does is leave an aftermath of feelings. These feelings overwhelm my chest. It's a deep aching of loss, yearning, and excitement all at once.

● ● ●

They fight for dominance to see which one is going to be stronger. This battle causes a pulsing of energy to radiate through my chest, from the middle of it outwards. It gives me a feeling of not being able to breathe.

Keeping my hands in place to hold up my head, I take several deep breaths to dispel the rising panic. As my descent into the unknown overwhelming feelings continues, my phone makes a noise. The notification is a blessing and a curse at the same time. It allows me to concentrate on something else, anything else, than this feeling that can easily drown me before the day starts.

I reach for the small electronic device, noticing the reduced aching pressure as I work the buttons. It's from Skylar. The panic and feeling of loss begin to return from the previous moment. Regardless of the mixed emotions running rampant inside of me, I smile sincerely. If anyone had been in the room with me, they would have said I looked like a fool.

I click on the message, my goofy smile still in place.

Skyler: Morning! How did you sleep?

Me: I had some interesting dreams. I am not entirely sure I was sleeping.

Skylar: But that one dream was enjoyable. I wouldn't mind a repeat of it.

I touch my lips softly with my fingertips, remembering moments ago what I was experiencing.

Me: I wouldn't mind either.

My response is honest, risky, and flirty. Skylar doesn't have a reply right away. It temporarily makes me question if it was the wrong thing to say. My insecurities start to creep in. This girl is causing so many different emotions that I have never had to deal with before. Without her, I feel like I'm drowning in desperation and self-loathing. That's not who I am or how I handle anything in my life.

I need to accept that Skylar means something to me, more than other people before her. I need to accept that no matter what I think or try to prevent, there's an authentic connection between us. Even if I don't fully understand what that connection originates from, it's impossible to will such strong feelings from out of existence. To continue with my life, I need to accept that I genuinely like her, regardless of my continued mental objection.

As I am self-analyzing, I miss that she has responded. I snap out of my thoughts to read what she sent to me.

Skylar: Will you go out to dinner with me tonight?

Me: I am not huge on eating dinner out or dinner in general. What about going out for dessert?

Skylar: It just so happens that dessert is my favorite part of the day.

Me: There are some things I need to get done today, but I will text you the place later.

Skylar: *kissing emoji* Can't wait.

Smiling at my phone, I set it down and take a breath. I'm incredibly excited to finally go on a date with her after hanging out for so many days. Uncle will not be happy about it, though.

Uncle, I forgot about him.

I pause, looking at the time. The clock shows it's midmorning. I have been neglecting my duties with him. Since working those extra shifts, my visits with him have been fewer and far between. I get up to dress quickly and see him. This is not going to be fun.

Chapter: 18

When I arrive at Uncle's shop, he finishes up with a customer, handing over a bag. I can't gauge what kind of mood he is in due to him smiling at the customer. I patiently wait for him to finish up.

The customer leaves, putting the two of us alone together in the room. He shuts the register to conclude the sale, and I wait for him to show me he's ready to talk. For a second, he stares at it. He's upset. I put on a hopeful but apprehensive smile.

Uncle turns to me. "Where have you been?" he asks in an unusually calm voice.

"I told you I was picking up more shifts at work for a little bit."

He maintains the same stance and tone of voice, "Yes, you did. That didn't mean you wouldn't still train at a different time of day or stop communicating for that duration."

I soften my voice at his concern, "I'm sorry, Uncle. I didn't mean to make you worry. I've just been preoccupied. We can train now if you want."

Uncle huffs slightly, "I can't right now. There are things in the shop that need to be addressed. Just come back tonight after dinner like you normally do."

Apprehension develops in my stomach when I answer, "I have plans tonight. I won't be able to make our normal time."

He looks at me with confusion, "I thought you told me you didn't have to work tonight."

This is the part of the conversation that veers into troubling territory.

I brace myself to the best of my ability for the conversation ahead. Looking as unfazed as possible, I answer him, "I don't work tonight."

Uncle's face still holds the same look of confusion, "Then why are you telling me you have plans?"

I stand straighter against the counter, "I have a date."

Uncle is taken aback by my answer, "You never told me you were dating. What's his name?"

I don't skip a beat, "HER name is Skylar. I just started dating. It is all rather new to me right now. The reason you weren't made aware of it has everything to do with me not knowing how to talk to you about this topic."

He is clearly upset by this. It's unclear if it is at himself or at what I said, "We have always had a relationship of open communication. About how you are feeling and how to deal with it while still protecting yourself. How is this any different?"

I sigh, "It is different because my entire life you have taught me to hide who I am, or at least a side of me, from others. The act of dating is literally to connect with another person, whoever they may be. I shouldn't have to be alone even if I think you will disapprove of what I am doing."

Uncle stares at me. He appears to be allowing what I'm saying to him to soak in. I can almost physically feel the cogs in his mind turning. They are running through different responses and scenarios before continuing his side of the conversation.

He says the next several sentences with more calm than before, "I always knew you would at some point start dating. The question wasn't "if", it was "when". I will always be your top supporter of what you do, but I will always be the first to protect you from untrustworthy people. This girl you have a date with, what do you know about her? This Skylar?"

I get a little annoyed with this line of conversation. Uncle is telling me that he is on my side while at the same time saying that I am not careful enough. The way he is addressing the situation with Skylar makes me defensive.

"I may not know everything about Skylar, but she allows me to be me without feeling bad. If talking about something makes me feel uncomfortable, she gives me the space I need. She doesn't push it. Knowing if someone is trustworthy is not always a snap judgment of character. That is why dating exists, for people to see if other characters are trustworthy and consistent. I don't mind being alone and spending my life with you and Melanie right now. But I am human, and I don't want to be alone forever. Especially if I find another person that gets me, even if there are secrets that need to be hidden," I say.

Uncle's face floods with sadness at my words. Me saying these things isn't meaning to hurt his feelings. It's to be honest with him about the situation. He wanted the conversation when I brought up the topic, but I'm not sure this is where he wants it to go. Thinking back through the years, not once do I remember him having anyone over. I don't remember him saying he was going out to meet other people or go on dates. Uncle is not a bad looking guy. Even with our life being unusual, he could have found someone to spend time with. The way he talks about trustworthiness, he never connected well with others. Was it because of me? Did I prevent him from living his life?

Any annoyance I'm feeling towards him dulls down immediately. It is a possibility that I'm the only person in his life. Looking at my Uncle's face, I can tell he wants to say something on the topic but may not know-how.

Given the current situation, I take the time to ask what is stuck on my tongue, "Did I prevent you from having a real life? A family of your own?"

Uncle smiles at me affectionately. He approaches me, stopping close enough to pat the top of my hand, "I'm doing what I want to be doing in life. You didn't prevent anything for me. I am right where I want to be."

My head moves in a light nod directed towards his response. I may want a companion, but that doesn't mean Uncle ever wanted one. I need to accept that sometimes, we have these arguments because what I want out of life is different from what he wants. The discussions and disagreements come from differences in perspectives. There is no changing either of ours. The only thing I can do is respect the difference.

I smile back at him, "Did you want me to stay with you in the store today?"

"No, I will be fine by myself today. You should go home to get ready for your date tonight. Please be careful," Uncle answers before moving from the counter to a stock of inventory still in boxes.

I give him a small wave goodbye, "Okay, see you Saturday night."

It's too early to get ready to see Skylar. I decide to run and get some coffee from my favorite spot.

The day is warm, coupled with complementary clear skies. Sitting at an outside café table, drinking coffee seems appropriate and relaxing for the afternoon.

Sitting at my usual table for roughly an hour allows for enough time to plan the evening. The entire trip is used to plot out what clothes to try on and how to do my hair.

Returning home from my afternoon, I sift around my clothes, pondering options. Each shirt is put with blue jeans to check compatibility, which is how I found myself in front of four options hanging off the closet door. In blue jeans and a black bra.

I pick up the first option, going for the bold red shirt. It's in the style of a halter. It has a zipper up the side to get on and off. Although it makes me feel rather sassy, it is not the best choice for a first date. I remove the shirt to place on the bed in the no section.

The next one that ends up on me is my rose shirt with a v neck. It is classy and sexy at the same time. It would be an excellent choice to wear to a meal or a concert, but it doesn't fit what I'm looking to achieve. Looking back at my other two options, I sigh.

The third one that I put on is a basic black tank top. I enjoy a black tank top just like the next person, and it looks good with anything. I'm staring at my reflection a bit longer, trying to predict how the evening will go with my non-psychic abilities— picturing her face in my mind.

I make the decision immediately that this shirt isn't good enough. The tank top goes on the growing pile of shirts.

The final and fourth design I try on is a turquoise sleeveless shirt with black ribbon laced up either side. It isn't overbearing, but it is stylish. It's my favorite shirt. I smile wide; this is the one I'm going to wear.

With the significant decision over, I send a quick text over to Skylar with the address of where we will be meeting in just a short amount of time. She sends back a heart in recognition.

Heading to the hair straightener in the bathroom, I turn it on to heat. While I'm waiting for it, I start my makeup. I take the same turquoise color in eye shadow for a small amount of extra accent, brushing it along my eyelids. With that confidently finished, I look at the borderline forgotten hair straightener. I part my hair in several large sections and start removing the waves from my strands.

About twenty minutes later, I feel like I am put together enough in all areas. That is until looking at the clock and seeing that I still have an hour until the meetup time. My mood goes from super confident to anxious rather quickly.

* * *

"Damn it," I say to myself before plopping down in my chair.

Wishing in that second, time would have moved slightly faster.

My nerves don't give me the luxury of remaining calm before the meetup time. It feels like someone is taking a thin rope from inside me and twisting it in circles. Each minute that passes seems to cause the cord to bunch upon itself, giving more tension. This feels like the worst kind of torture, the waiting. I grab my things and go out, leaving my current prison.

As soon as the outside world is within my vision, the building tension releases slightly, melting away. To help with the rest of the anxiousness, I head to the meeting spot.

Arriving fifteen minutes early, I take a seat near a window. Inside, customers are finishing their dinners. I hear some ordering desserts while others are paying to leave. By the time Skylar will arrive, there will be fewer people with less noise. I let the waitress know that another person is coming.

Leaning back in the chair, I pick up the menu to review. My eyes sweep over each item like I haven't been here several times before. In this situation, they feel new to me.

Finally, I have it narrowed down to two choices. I lift my head to look around me. Looking out the window, I do a double-take seeing Skylar approaching. She is looking around, giving me a second to look at her.

* * *

She has her hair in a half-up style. Around her neck is a black ribbon choker. Her shirt is a wrap design of a sunset orange. The shirt is paired with black jeans and tan ankle boots, complete with a black accent bracelet on her left wrist. She looks hardcore, carefree, and sexy all at once.

Grabbing my phone quickly, I text her that I'm already inside at a table. As soon as the text is sent, my eyes immediately go to her.

There I witness Skylar reach for her phone, take a second to read it, and smile. With the phone still in her hand, she moves to the entrance doors.

I get up from my seat quickly to meet her. My introduction coming out slightly awkward, "Hey, we're seated over there,"

She smiles with excitement, motioning for me to go first, "I'll follow your lead then."

Before moving, my eyes can't help but look her over once more causing me to blurt out, "You look lovely."

She lightly laughs, then slowly does a look over of me, "You don't look so bad yourself."

Her unashamed flirting and directness slightly frazzle me. I'm lucky enough to be in front, walking us to the table. Otherwise, she would see the blush written all over my face.

Skylar gets settled into her seat, picking up a menu, "I see we were both early tonight."

"Better to be early rather than late, I say. More time to be prepared."

"Are you?"

"Am I what?" I look up from my menu to find her looking at me, intent on getting her answer. I feel like she is looking for something inside of me.

"More prepared from arriving earlier," she responds to me in an explanation.

I shrug my shoulders and smile at her, "The only thing I feel like I'm more prepared about is what I want to order."

She turns her eyes back to the itemized food list, "That sounds much further than me indeed. What do you suggest I order?"

"That depends on your mood. I can tell you the dessert cakes are extremely good, though."

Skylar just nods her head, contemplating the options. The waitress arrives shortly after that to take our order. I end up going for the strawberry cream cake, with Skylar getting the sticky chocolate cake.

A small silence settles between us but free of the previous awkward feelings. We seem to be in our minds reflecting staring at each other.

I'm the one who ends up breaking the silence, "You know, I just realized something. You spent weeks coming to visit me at my job, but I don't know what you do. I know you don't' always like to follow the rules, which sometimes gets you in trouble. But not what your work and career are."

My honest, observant statement of her character rewards me with a shy smile. It's small and apprehensive. I file that away in my mind to be part of who Skylar's character truly is, not who she thinks I want her to be. There's nothing I want more at this moment than to break down her walls and know her, the real her.

Skylar fiddles with her glass of water while she responds, "My career and work are not easily categorized. What I do is very freelance. My clients usually deal with unusual requests or need something that many platform services can't provide. It's a very diverse field. But I like it because I make my own hours and can get things done my way."

"Well…that sounds very impressive and creepy at the same time. I wasn't sure that was possible." Skylar's head is thrown back in a deep laugh. The action puts a large smile on my face.

When her laughing calms down, she looks at me with her eyes lit up, "I can understand why you would say that. Freelancing can be an obscure scene. What did you think I did?"

I made a thoughtful face thinking back to my theories, "Honestly, I thought you were a lawyer or something office related, like HR. Anything else seems like a waste of your personality. Now that you told me Freelancing, that seems to fit you better than a lawyer. Either way, you stand up for what you believe in, aren't shy about what you want, and follow through to the end."

Skylar's small shy smile shows up again. Like she is trying to hold back something from coming out.

At that moment, our desserts are brought out. It's great timing because I'm not sure where to take that conversation next. I'm a bit more open than usual tonight. This probably has a lot to do with Skylar being more honest with me. But that doesn't mean all my walls could go down.

Skylar takes a bite of her cake, humming her appreciation of its flavors. Which almost makes me choke on mine, causing me to reach for my water.

"This is good!" She says.

I look at her questioning, "Have you never had sticky chocolate cake before?"

She eats another piece, "No, this is the first time."

I'm taken aback by her statement, "I'm surprised. Did your mom not let you eat desserts growing up?"

What I just said makes her pause. Without realizing it, I hit something personal to her. I guess we are more alike than I thought when it comes to talking about family.

When she answers, she is picking at the cake with her fork, "Growing up, there weren't a lot of desserts that we ate. There were certain rules that were extremely strict, and that was one of them," there is a pause before she looks up at me smiling sweetly, "but I am glad I get to do this with you right now."

I take a second to look over her face, digesting what she just told me. Don't just stare at her. Say something to make her feel more comfortable!

"Well, in that case, I'm delighted that we are doing this together now as well."

That causes her to reach out to place her hand over mine, "I've never met someone quite like you, Selena."

Warmth fills my heart at her touch and words. I feel a light buzz of energy exchanging between our hands. My mind is reminded of our dream last night and how intimate we were. I see her eyes flick to my lips for a second. She removes her hand to finish eating her cake. Looking at my now empty plate, then outside at the sun's last lights falling behind the horizon. The realization is quickly forming that I didn't want this evening to end here.

"Thank you, Skylar. Do you want to go for a walk around the city after this?" I ask, feeling somewhat vulnerable.

Skylar looks to be emitting an aura of happiness when she answers, "I would love to."

I motion to the waitress that we were ready to finish up. As she brought over a paper for me to sign, I saw Skylar reaching to get some cash. I finish filling out the credit card receipt and, the waitress and I exchange the items in our hands.

● ● ●

"I already paid for the meal Skylar, don't worry about any of it."

She looks at me confused, cash still in hand, "How did you pay so quickly?"

I cover my mouth laughing, "I gave the waitress my card before you arrived and told her to run everything on it when we were finishing up eating."

Skylar put her money back in her pocket, "That is very impressive. Although I asked you, so I should have paid."

I wink at her, then get up out of my chair to whisper in her ear in passing, "It's okay. I used the tip money you gave me all those nights working. I thought it was only fair."

Skylar's face turns red right before I move to exit the building with her behind me.

Chapter: 19

I hold the outer door open for Skylar to exit the building. The air has grown slightly cooler with a light breeze going. It's hard to tell if it is going to rain or not. I toe the street on the sidewalk, looking back and forth to see what kind of traffic is going on. It's light considering the time. With it being a Thursday night, nothing extraordinary appears to be going on.

I turn my head to see Skylar next to me with her eyes closed, face up to the sky, and breathing in deeply. I just watch her. I don't say anything to disrupt this moment, and I just watch her enjoying something only she knows.

When she is ready, she opens her eyes. Looking at me smiling, "Ready?"

"Always," I answer.

Skylar steps off the curve to cross the street, heading to another that pulls off the traffic's primary road. I follow close behind her. She slows down to wait for me. We soon fall into a comfortable pace.

Looking at me sideways, she voices her thoughts, "So I have a question that has been bothering me."

Surprisingly enough, I don't feel alarmed or panicked by her random statement. I feel a large amount of calmness before answering, "Sure, go ahead."

She pauses, then asks me with a conviction that shows she has spent real time thinking about this question, "Why do you work in a bar?"

Her question immediately makes me burst out laughing, "That is what has been bothering you? Of all the questions you have, that's the one keeping you up at night? I work in a bar for several reasons. My boss Joe respects my differences, I get to meet and talk to new people without over committing to them, and when people drink, they tip me more so I can make a lot of money."

"But don't you want a career that will provide more security for you?" she pries a bit further.

I think about it for a second before answering, "My job is pretty secure. I may not have the benefits that some other jobs do, but it fits me right now. Who knows about the future. Maybe I'll do something different."

She seems to accept my response, contemplating and mulling it over. Finally, she says, "I can understand that," there is a pause before she continues, "Plus, your ass looks super sexy in your jeans when you work."

I scoff, pretending like that statement didn't mean everything to me. I playfully push Skylar to the side, "Are you creepily staring at my ass when I'm working?"

Her laugh is flirty as she immediately fires back at me, "Like you don't stand there staring at me when I'm not looking at you."

She creates a carefree environment around us as we walk next to each other, making me feel utterly relaxed and open. No place on this Earth has ever made me feel the way I do right now.

I put both my hands up like she caught me doing something, "Fine, fine. You got me. You're right. I do stare at you when you aren't looking."

She seems to take the honest confession as an endearment because she steps closer, intertwining her fingers with mine, "There's nothing wrong with that, though."

My heart jumps at her movement not only because of her connection to me but from how close she is. I lightly squeeze her hand in mine, looking into her blue eyes, "No, there is nothing wrong with that."

We fall into step with each other, and easy conversation flows between us about likes and dislikes. About passions and hobbies. Nothing heavy about family, childhoods, or past relationships. Our walk is carefree.

That is, until we hear a voice call out, "Hey!"

When we hear the intrusion, Skylar is mid-sentence. Both of us are smiling at each other. My reflexes are slower from being so at ease with her. My smile falls. I look around to who is calling out. What I find is a male and female across the street moving towards us.

I look over at Skylar. Her face shows that she is not amused with the intrusion either. My body tensing as she lets go of my hand. Skylar's movement ends with the crossing of her arms in front of her.

As they stop in front of us, I can't help the attitude that comes out of me, "Can we help you?"

The guy barely gives me the time of day. The female is the one that talks first, "Skylar, our boss is wondering what is taking so long. The job is supposed to be complete already."

All the openness and relaxation are gone from her now, "Okay, several things. One, I told everyone I'm off tonight. Two, I told everyone I would get it done on my time. Three, for gods' sakes, I have a cell phone. Is stomping through the street at me seriously necessary?"

The girl has the decency to shrug her shoulders in partial embarrassment, "He told us to follow up."

I would have laughed at how comically these two were having it handed to them right now if it wasn't for how upset Skylar seemed. Reacting off of Skylar, my instincts are going into gear. Ready to strike if I need to but waiting to see what happens. I'm surveying my surroundings, the street names nearby at the intersection up ahead. We're about two or three blocks from my apartment building. We walked far.

Skylar's getting angrier by the second. She throws out her hands in an overview motion to encompass the present area and raises her voice, "He told you to follow up? Like this though?? REALLY? You guys have no brains."

The guy doesn't seem to like what she says to them very much, "You need to come in to speak with him. He wants to talk to you in person."

She isn't budging. Skylar stands up straighter than before to continue to look the guy right in the eyes, "I will call him tomorrow to discuss our agreement."

"No, you are going to talk to him now," he moves forward with his hand grabbing her left forearm forcibly. This action triggers something in me I never dealt with before. A feeling of surging rage to defend what is mine overcomes me.

What follows after that, I'm not entirely even sure. All I know is that the guy tried to force Skylar to go with him making me move into action. I remove his hand from her arm, and then there is fighting.

I'm aggressively fighting the guy. At some point, I see Skylar fighting the girl who, I assume, is trying to back him up. Both the newcomers end up on the sidewalk rolling around in pain.

I grab Skylar's hand pulling her, into a run. She follows without question. Before getting too far, my eyes spare a look back at the pair still on the sidewalk. They won't be able to get up for a couple of minutes easily. Pulling Skylar around several corners, she manages to keep up with me while I direct us back to my place. Adrenaline is slamming through my veins. At this moment, it's clear that Skylar has some defense skills. Otherwise, she would not have been able to hold her own and would potentially be freaking out right now.

Arriving at my building, we climb the three flights of stairs up. When we arrive at my door, I somehow get us inside it without breaking it down or slamming it shut. We are both severely out of breath, leaning our backs on the now closed door. There is no way that those two could follow us here. We were too far ahead of them.

I look around the well-known space but somehow, it feels different. I catch a part of my appearance on a reflective surface. My eyes were projecting their green hue. No, no, no. It would have been too late to explain everything that just happened to Skylar. The only thing I can think to do is apologize. The time for fear has long passed us in the street. The only thing I have left at this moment is to accept whatever is about to happen from my choice to defend her.

My voice comes out feeling stuck in my throat as I close my eyes, resting the back of my head on the closed door, "Skylar…I…"

Before I can finish what I'm trying to say, I feel her hand on my chin. She's no longer next to me but in front of me. Skylar's voice sounds different when she commands me, "Selena look at me."

I don't immediately comply. Mentally accepting and physically acting are two different things. I was only human after all. Skylar has to ask me again, but the second time sounds more like a plea. I open my eyes, lifting my head. Skylar is now the only thing in my vision. I see her beautiful face with her very own eyes glowing blue hue.

It produces a gasp from me. I want to cry; I want to yell. So many questions and feelings enter my being, but my mouth can't seem to communicate any of them. We remain there with her close enough to be holding my chin, staring at each other. She is like me; she is like me.

The next thing I know, our bodies are clashing together in an explosion of colorful energy—our lips on each other in a fever. My back is still against the door, but Skylar's hand is now around my neck. My hands are frantically pulling her closer to me.

All my senses are overloaded. I'm not sure where the start or end of anything is. I can't tell what feelings belong to Skylar or me. Her teeth are nipping with different levels of intensity at my bottom lip, ear lobe, and neck. Our embrace is a million times better than any dream we have had. We were starving for each other.

My hands end up under her shirt, all over her stomach, sides, and back. I'm unable to settle on just one area. The feeling of her silky skin under my hands fueling me forward. I start pushing her away from the front door to the bedroom. Skylar's hands move into my hair with her nails scraping against my scalp. Whenever she digs her nails into my upper neck and scalp, mine automatically do the same. We move as one unit around the living room, circling, keeping equal balance as much as possible. It's a back and forth of control.

The short journey to the bedroom is trailed by our shoes, shirts, and pants littering the floor and furniture. In the room, Skylar's body hits the mattress first. We both take off each other's underwear, rolling back and forth in a flurry of kisses and heat. The battle for the top ends with me pushing her against the bed. I immediately straddle her and pin her wrists down.

Skylar is breathing heavily under me. I kiss down the middle of her chest between her breasts. Without warning, I bite the top of her right breast. She lets out a surprised gasp, pushing against my hands on her wrists. My mouth releases the captured flesh to reveal a developing purple bruise.

The forces from her wrists that are asking for me to release them from my hand's stop. Moving to the other breast, I bite the top again. Skylar is no longer surprised but still pushes against my hands to touch me. I continue to hold them in place, biting down harder. My knee goes between her legs, leaning forward. Any noises of pain, she is making changes to noises of pleasure. I let go of her wrists, giving in to her non-verbal request.

Her hands react quickly. Skylar's fingertips and nails are dragging down my back. Her knee comes up against me. I brace my hands on either side of her head for balance. With my focus changing, Skylar starts her own biting. She matches the marks I make on her and more. She's taking advantage of my position to find the hard and soft spots on my upper chest. I have no control over the noises I'm making. When she lets go to kiss me heatedly, one of my hands goes into her hair to pull it. My frustration is showing itself if I mean to or not.

Both our hips are moving, and heat is radiating from our pores. Our bodies are communicating with each other through noises and movements. My leg retracts from Skylar's moving hips to be replaced by my right hand, where she wants me most. With my fingers working deliberately, my knee moves behind my hand to add pressure. Skylar matches my movements. Our bodies move in unison like a sweet symphony playing with different highs and lows from that point on. We are moving to varying speeds of the metronome.

Skylar and I possess each other's energy, soul, and body. For what seems like hours, we do this until exhaustion replaces the starving feeling. Soon after, we fall asleep. Skylar ends up with her arm around my waist and her face resting on my breast. My fingertips play lightly with her beautiful hair. A deep peace fills me. A peace I have never felt in my life with any other lover. The sound of her leveling breath soothes me into a lull of sleep.

Chapter: 20

When I wake the next morning, the feeling of peace remains in me. My eyes stay shut for a moment longer, reveling in the sense of completeness that fills my heart and soul. It's hard to understand that one person can make me feel this way.

I slowly open them, observing slivers of light coming into the room, playing on the wall. Laying on my side, I take in Skylar's sleeping form while she's on her back. The feeling of wanting to reach out to run my hands over her skin is monumental. Somehow, I refrain from doing so to bask in her sleeping glow a little while longer.

I have to accept that the more I fight to keep how I feel about this beautiful woman next to me at bay, the more it will hurt me. Each denial I make causes deep anxiety that, at some point, becomes unbearable. There's no way to fight against this anymore, something that came so naturally to us. A connection that is so unlike any I felt before. I needed to accept that controlling many things is an option in life, but

* * *

this isn't one of them. Even with all of the training I have in my life, nothing could have prepared me for this.

Not only is it about our apparent connection, but it's also about the fact that her eyes glow too. A part of me knew I couldn't be the only one in the world that's like this. It isn't like I can actively ask people if they have unusual strength, and their eyes glow weird colors. That would have been a one-way ticket to a psych ward or prison cell. Uncle's the only one I can talk to about these feelings and the issues I encountered growing up. At the end of the day, though, he may know about it, but he can never personally experience it himself. Knowing I can talk to her about it thaws something deep inside me that I didn't realize was even blocked off.

My hand reaches out to lightly go through her hair. I have to finally admit to myself that Skylar had my heart from the very first time she came into my dreams all those nights ago. My fingers lightly run over the side of her face. Skylar's eyes flutter open, a smile slowly spreading across her lips. She leans into my touch, showing her affection. I continue to caress her, moving my fingertips to her upper chest lightly.

Softly whispering to her, "Morning." She turns her face to look at me. Every wall of hers is down, and every emotion is evident for me to read.

She responds to me without pause, "Morning."

Skylar moves the rest of her body to face me. I rest my hand on the bed between us. We stare at each other, just remaining in this bubble until I break it.

"We should talk about last night," I say.

Her face turns partially cocky from a deflective defense, but it lacks the proper conviction, "You mean how awesome it was."

My hand goes back to her face, softly touching her. I move my thumb just under her eyes, causing her to close them. Then move it to outline her bottom lip back and forth, "No. I mean, yes. It was awesome. But no, about how I've never met someone like me before. My whole life, a part of me has felt alone."

Skylar looks into my eyes with understanding, "There is no one like you, Selena. I understand what you mean more than you know. Maybe not to the degree you're describing. But the feeling of not being able to talk to people about how you feel or what you are experiencing. It can make you feel lost and imperfect at times, no matter how strong we are."

Skylar, I'm learning quickly, is one of the strongest people I know. Not just because of how capable of a person she is, but because she doesn't always let her ego run what she's doing. In one of the most vulnerable moments of my life, she met me with her own matched vulnerability.

The next words I say seem to have a life of their own, "Skylar, you always felt perfect to me the way you are. With me discovering how much you mean to me, it makes me feel less lost."

I visually watch as my words knock whatever weak defense she still has in place down.

What she says next comes out sounding like an airy wish, "I love you."

After saying it, she looks like she is about to cry. Moving as close as I can to her, I take her face in both my hands. It noticeably takes great effort for her to overcome something she is battling inside. Several tears are falling that I brush away with each of my thumbs. Moving my face to hers, my lips kiss her in an action that is confident but sensual. That is comforting and reassuring.

"I love you too. Please don't cry. You are too cute to be sad," I say before peppering kisses all over Skylar's face and shoulders. This action causes her to laugh. She pushes me onto my back, effectively rolling us over. She sits on my waist, wrapping her arms around me in a tight cocoon. Her lips meet mine in a kiss that is full of emotions, mental hopes, and future wishes.

I hear a phone vibrate, but it's further away. Skylar whines mid-kiss. When she pulls back from me, she is smiling, reaching for her phone.

Everything changes when she picks up the phone to see who is calling her. In one moment, her face falls, her body goes tense on top of me, and she becomes closed off.

I decide to probe a little, "Is everything okay?"

She is already typing a message to whoever contacted her, dismissing my question, "Yeah, it's just my family," she rolls off me to get out of the bed and walks to the bedroom door, "I need to call them real quick."

There isn't a lot to say since I'm now feeling slightly alert to her emotions, "Sure."

She disappears into the living room to make her call. I remain as I am. The small bubble that was temporarily built around us popped. We said we loved each other. The shock of the event isn't a lot. It's more of a calm reality, calm acceptance. It seems appropriate to match all these revelations that are happening within me. I don't say it very often, but in this case with her, I feel it. What I know is that my soul has a connection to hers.

Skylar's voice elevates in volume slightly but not loud enough for me to hear what she's saying. She seems to be fighting with whomever she is speaking with on the phone. I remain where I am to continue giving her the space she needs. Both hands behind my head, waiting to see what's coming once she comes back into the room.

I only have to wait five more minutes to find out. Skylar comes back to the door frame leaning her shoulder against it, sighing deeply. She doesn't immediately speak; I don't directly ask anything. Skylar just stays there with her phone in her hands, staring at it. I remain silent, waiting, and leaving her the room for any communication when she's ready, with no added pressure. Skylar crosses her arms in front of her, looking at me.

What comes out of her mouth sounds like a person devoid of emotion, "My family wants to meet you."

I raise my eyebrows, "Really? You don't seem to like them very much."

"I don't like them, but they are my family, and they are asking to meet you. I can avoid them but not forever. When I make their life difficult, they make my life difficult."

I watch her as she talks to me. She gives nothing away. The only way for me to take it is at face value. What we are discussing right now is evidently a very serious conversation, but a part of me wants to laugh. Skylar's attitude and stance are tense, but she's standing there naked. Against the door frame covered in multiple bruises that I graced her skin several hours before. It's almost comical.

I respond in a neutral voice, "Okay."

Skylar mimics me, "Okay."

I keep it as simple as possible, "When?"

"Are you free today?"

"I usually work these nights, but it just so happens that I'm off. So, I'm free."

"Is early evening okay?"

I smile at her awkwardness right now. She is acting like we didn't just bear our souls to each other mere moments ago. That call clearly threw her off. I answer her, "Sure, whenever works fine."

Skylar is on her phone typing quickly, "I will communicate that. I'm going to go take care of some things beforehand." She turns to move towards the front door, still typing.

I chuckle to myself. Skylar is so cute even when she's frustrated by her family. I casually get out of the bed to stand where she was just leaning against the doorway. I shout after her, "Skylar." She doesn't answer or stop right away. I laugh out loud and call after her louder, "Skylar!"

Skylar locking her phone, turns to look at me, "What?"

"You're naked."

She returns to reality when she let's what I say to her sink in. By this point, I'm walking towards her. She immediately starts laughing uncontrollably. When I reach her, a large playful smile encompasses my face from Skylar laughing so hard. I take her phone from her hand, tossing it. Pushing her against the front door, she lets out a soft hiss from the cool temperature on her skin.

I lean in to kiss her deeply, letting her know I understand her frustration. At first, I feel her holding back, but she lets go to match my intensity soon after.

When we pull away, she looks into my eyes, "I need to leave to get ready."

I nod my head in recognition holding her gaze, "I love you."

Skylar's face changes to the softness I knew last night and this morning when she answers my verbal call, "I love you." She moves forward again, our lips meeting. This time the kiss is different than before. Skylar is now showing me her love, desperation, and fear. I push back letting her know I hear her.

I pull her away from the door as I step aside, "Go get your stuff and get ready for today."

She hesitates a second to search out her clothes, wanting to linger there with me longer. My head moves to indicate for her to continue, causing her to move without any doubt. As she finds one clothing article after another to put back on, I take temporary residence in my chair, watching her peacefully.

Now fully dressed, Skylar recollects her phone. Her hand now on the doorknob to leave. Before opening the door, Skylar turns to me, "I'll see you shortly. I know you have a lot of questions. I promise some of them will get answered soon."

She smiles sweetly at me after saying it. Skylar's smile prompts me to give her a small wave in departure. She shakes her head at me in amusement. Then she opens the door and leaves.

My apartment immediately feels less without her. Regardless, my smile remains because I found someone who understands me without words. It isn't a one-night stand like others. We see each other's souls. She promised that I would get answers soon, so I decided to trust her. By meeting her family, maybe I'll be able to answer my questions about who I am and why I'm different. I got up from my chair to prepare for the very unusual day ahead of me.

Skylar texts me a couple of hours later to let me know where we are meeting and the time. We are going to an area of the city I have never seen before. On the way, we talk about random things and laughing at awful pick-up lines we've heard in the past. Skylar is a person I love, and I know that now. But regardless of how happy I feel, a foreboding feeling is sneaking in. Is this my instinct kicking in from my training or just anxiety? Uncle always told me to trust my gut in every situation.

My left-hand remains in hers as we walk, but my eyes are ever vigilant, looking around. My multitasking skills are near perfect at this point in my life.

"It's just around the corner; it will be the red stone one," she says.

We round the corner to a small row of houses. While we continued towards our destination, my gut feeling becomes slightly panicked, causing my hand to tense slightly.

"Don't be nervous babe, they will love you," Skylar tries to reassure me, pausing slightly at the steps leading to the front door. She is trying to make me feel better, but at this point, we both seem different degrees of nervous. She lets go of my hand, goes to the door, and knocks. My feet climb the steps to be next to her. The door opens just as I kiss her on the cheek.

A gentleman of late middle age and dressed as a butler speaks, "Evening ma'am, the family is waiting for your company downstairs."

Skylar clears her throat, "Ah yes, hello Gregory. Thank you." I'm staring at the butler and then further into a surprisingly nice-looking home. I'm literally shocked. I can't help my mouth gaping open. She never told me she came from such a nice background. Every conversation we have had about her family was short and offhanded.

Gregory moves to the side to let us through, nodding his head to us as we pass the threshold. As he closes the door, the thought of now or never passes through my mind. She retakes my hand, effectively deciding for me. Skylar starts the journey through the house that only she knew—passing several closed doors, leading us through an open one to some stairs. The stairs descend, hugging the wall, and at the bottom spiraling out around a small stone column.

After descending the spiral stairs, a feeling of nervousness is fighting to come through my body. It only seems like Skylar makes it come out, yet comforts me at the same time. You can't appear weak in front of her family, put it aside, and be confident like the person you are. I straighten my back and put extra energy into my steps. I see her face turn towards me from the side of my view as I look around.

The wallpaper is red, and the floor is dark brown wood. There are decorative torches, heavy-looking with an old-style to them, sitting above our heads. The hallway is not very wide, barely fitting two people next to each other. It could either be a great advantage or a flaw in defense, depending on which side you are on.

The foyer seems decent in length, with two doors at the end. The word door is putting it weakly. This entranceway is the most magnificent piece of wood I have ever seen. The design is thicker wood than most doors I have seen anywhere. The wood itself is a light brown that compliments the red walls and the darker wooden floor. Covering both doors are engravings of people, animals, and what looks to be buildings. It seems like some kind of scene playing out. The door handles are black forged iron castile.

We reach the mammoth entryway.

Skylar pauses in front of it, "This is the room that my family likes to meet in."

"Seems weird that it resembles a fortress."

Skylar just shrugs her one shoulder and doesn't verbally respond. Her hand goes to the door handle and rests on it. She is still holding my hand, and my anxiety is trying not to smother me. I look at her, but her face seems void of any emotion, the tension visible from her muscles. Maybe the anxiety isn't mine?

I lightly squeeze her hand to try to reassure her. She opens the door to a vast open room with beautiful marble pillars throughout, looming from floor to ceiling.

There are several people in the room. At the other end are several stairs to a platform with one chair on it, similar to a throne. Partially in the room, closer to the chair, is a red-carpet runner that travels up the stairs to the chair's front. She lets go of my hand, walking forward to the group of people whose stares show that they judge me. I put some of my charms in place, giving a small smile. My sight is no longer filling with the room we are in but the people in front of me. There's an array of emotions showing on the faces in front of me. My primary purpose right now is to get these people not to hate me.

Skylar starts talking to some of the people in front of us, making introductions. In the background, I hear the door open and several footsteps.

Then a loud clap resounds through the room, "At last! She has arrived! Now we can really get the party started," a male voice rings out.

Skylar tenses, and the group collectively turns their heads towards the man talking. The group of people part down the middle to reveal a face I never wanted to see again. Ryder. And he is sitting on the throne.

Chapter: 21

Ryder has a nice suit on and a tie of red stripes. Next to him stands a younger man with similar features, which I assume is his brother.

I narrow my eyes at him, "You have got to be kidding me."

He gives a wide Cheshire cat smile, "I assure you, Selena, dear, there is no kidding. I have been trying to get you in here for some time, but we had to make sure you were who we thought you were."

I quickly look over to Skylar when he says this. She isn't looking at me but straight ahead, with no emotion. What did she do?

"Color me not impressed." I snap back. Several people around me snicker.

"You still ended up here in the end anyway," he says with his smugness shining.

I laugh loudly at him, "Not from anything you did, believe me. I ended up giving you entirely way too much of my attention from the start, for far longer than needed." Again I hear people around me snicker.

His face quickly falls into a scowl. I could have sworn I heard him even growl a little bit. "The only reason I tried at all was to find out who you were," he said.

I look at Skylar still standing next to me, her head is down looking at the floor, "Are you related to this jerk?"

As soon I ask this question, Ryder looks pleased I bring it up. He calls out in a commanding voice, "Skylar," motioning her to come to him. I take notice that Skylar leaves my side to go to him without hesitation. The people standing around us in a small crowd move away from the area—leaving me alone. Feeling alone and abandoned without support, all I can do is watch her walk to him. Skylar climbs the small stairs to stand behind his chair, resting her right hand on the top. Her face is unreadable stone.

"I have a confession to make," he taps his fingers on his armrest. He's acting like we are best friends, and he is going to tell me something no one else knows, "The truth is I sent Skylar to you. I told her to get you here by any means necessary because I couldn't get what I needed from you. This meeting is a trap. At the end of the day, though, she is mine. We are engaged to be married."

I hear the words he is saying, but they don't process all the way. There is no way he's telling the truth, repeating what he's saying in my head, my memory flashes. It goes back to the work party where I saw her talking to Ryder, to previous conversations that Skylar and I had since I met her about her family, and this morning when she got that phone call. Yesterday, when we met the two thugs in the street trying to force her to meet with her boss, meet with Ryder. The night that led to a revelation for us both was a lie. With all the information I'm given now, it makes sense—a trap.

Once the shock of what he says wears off, the panic and raw emotions set in. My instincts are violently opposing each other. I want to run. I want to run and need to leave. I need fresh air. I physically can't move; my body refuses my brain's commands. My eyes and ears object to register what events are happening.
I need to escape, and I need to hit something, I need to do something.

My brain is out of control. Everything I put into training, mentally and physically, is shattering. All those years at this very moment feel entirely useless. The panic is quickly joined by pain and despair.

Why did I not see this coming? Why did I not heed the warnings on the way here? My heart is breaking. My lungs seem like they can't work on their own. I put my hand to my chest to try to regulate my heart and breathing better. Or just to see if my heart will come through my chest. Stay alive, stay alive, breathe.

● ● ●

During all of this, I neglected to pay attention to the area behind me. I feel sharp weapons making themselves known in my back and sides as I gain back my sense of control.

I estimate roughly three guards dressed like the people that attacked me both times in the streets. They are holding an assortment of spears and swords towards me. At one point surrounding me, the crowds of people were now in two smaller sections farther away on each side.

I look at Ryder and Skylar next to each other, one sitting and one standing. I look at Skylar in particular, "How could you? You said I was going to get answers but is this what you meant? Like this? This is not who you are."

She doesn't respond. She doesn't even look at me when I ask. I doubt Skylar is going to respond since she is clearly submissive to Ryder. How she's acting now isn't the person I know her to be. But it turns out I didn't know her at all. All my self-doubt and insecurities run through my mind.

Uncle taught me that showing emotions was a weakness that could be used against me. Unfortunately, all my reflexes from the past years are gone. I know my pain is written all over my face. I'm in the throws of what that long-ago lesson really means.

On Ryder's face now sits a small arrogant smile that is barely evident. Watching my feelings play out in front of him; he turns to look at Skylar next to him, "Look darling, she cares about you, how quaint."

When he says this, I can't bring myself to look towards her face. I fear I may in fact actually die. I have never heard any stories of ever dying from a broken heart. But in that second, I'm semi surprised it hasn't happened yet. Anger flares up, quickly joining its siblings to make a dangerous cocktail.

I look him right in the eye and say as deadpan as possible, "You put in a great effort and a lot of resources to get me to this point. So why?"

He raises his hand in an absent-minded effort looking at his brother first, then back to me, "Your existence is a threat to my family. That is why you were hidden in the first place."

"I am intelligent enough to figure out why I was hidden all these years by myself but thank you for the commentary. What I don't know is, why am I a threat?"

"It has to do with your blood and where it comes from," Ryder's annoyance at my questioning everything starts to show.

The longer I am forced to stand in my current spot in front of him, the angrier I get. My hands, now back to my sides, began to shake with my emotion. I know, at this point, my eyes are glowing. I feel my nerves on edge, which can be either my advantage or my weakness. I will end up making irrational decisions or have the confidence for hard choices.

"I am sorry that they didn't teach you basic knowledge. It seems brain-wise they failed you because my blood comes from my heart."

He laughs heartedly at my expense. His mocking of me makes me spring into action. I kick the guard to my right in the balls while grabbing the spear away from him. The guards behind and on the left move their spears to where I was while I roll away.

I spin around just as they push towards me again. I duck and wait for the whooshing noise feeling the wind pass above me. With the spear in my hand, I jam it up under the chin of the guard that is behind me. As I pull it out, I kick the other away from me, causing him to land several feet away. This weapon is my chance for the plan that, in reality, only had a 30 second life in my brain. I take my step and throw.

As my hand lets go of the spear, more guards are already tackling me to the floor. I know the weapon didn't hit my mark but there is screaming, so I hit someone. A moment of panic fills me, hoping I didn't hit her. The alarm is quickly replaced by anger and heartache once again when memories came back to my brain. She was never mine to worry about, even when I had her.

The guards punch and kick me, making me taste a hint of tangy metal in my mouth. They pick me up and confine me with my hands behind my back. I look up in that second, and she appears to be undamaged with her hands over her mouth, shock in her eyes. At least now she is feeling something. Obviously, my emotional turmoil isn't enough to get her to react.

My eyes then move to the others next to her. The spear decided to take home in the next best target, Ryder's brother. Who's just dropped to the floor with the spear protruding from his eye socket. Sweet justice, not my main target, but that works. I start laughing with what I can only assume is a slightly bloody smile.

He looks at me with pure anger, his eyes glowing red, "Take her to the dungeon. She dies tomorrow morning."

With my arms still restrained, I'm violently turned around and shoved towards a door on the left. The momentum makes me fall on my left shoulder. Crap, that hurt a bit. I look at Skylar one more time from the floor, then at Ryder, then over to his now-dead relative. I decide to leave them with one more parting present of chaos.

"You know Ryder, at the end of the day when you lay with her, she will always be thinking of me—thinking how I'm better than you. When she falls asleep, she will think of how she loves me more," I yell so the entire room can hear me.

In that second, I laugh harder than I have in a while. I get a kick to the ribs for it, which knocks the wind out of me. Two guards pick me up and take me past the door to the hall, my laughter starting up again at my own amusement.

Chapter: 22

The men surrounding me walk us through several doorways, then down another set of stairs. How many floors were in this building? Soon we are walking down a much longer hallway. The guard's grip on me is stiff, and they don't speak at all. There's one on either side of me holding my arm and two behind me. I weigh the options if it's worth fighting four people to escape, or should I wait for the night to fall? We reach two more guards in front of a door, which makes the decision for me to wait until dark. They look at me with curiosity and nod at the men holding me. I smile at them and blow them a kiss in the air. The one guard turns stern, and the other one smiles a bit.

We pass through the door into a room with blocks of cells. The cells have bars that are thicker than I would have thought. It looks like they are made of cast iron, giving the room the look of being from centuries past. There's a bench against the back wall in all the cells and not a ton of space inside. Two guards stay by the door, and the other two move me to the cell furthest into the room on the left. The door's opened by an old skeleton key. Before putting me in the cell, they take caste iron shackles off the wall.

"Really? This room doesn't seem very modern." I muse out loud. The guard immediately takes retribution for my comment by punching me in my side. As I buckle over, they grab my hands and put them in the shackle cuffs.

"You guys are assholes," I say, pushing the words past my lips as I try to pull more air into my lungs. They toss me forward into the cell, trying to make me off balance. I tuck and roll forward, turning on the upwards motion to sit on the bench. The guards quickly lock the door and step back. I smile and wave at them in my cuffs as they turn and leave without ever saying a word.

After they leave, it becomes hushed in the room. I can't hear any noise except the clanking of the chains holding me. I lean back against the wall and sigh.

"What the hell just happened?" I lift my hands to my face— the adrenaline wearing off accents the sore feelings around my body. My mind is replaying everything that happened almost an hour before.

I'm stuck in this situation from coming to visit Skylar's family. I came to keep her out of trouble and trusted she would guide me. She's my person, my heart, but it was all a trap.

* * *

This entire time, everything was preplanned. Ryder and Skylar dating me were a trap. They meant to kill me from the beginning of everything. The group of people that attacked me two separate times in the street was on purpose, to get me here by force.

This situation is what Uncle has been warning me about my entire life. But Skylar warmed my heart and made me trust her. With her beautiful blue eyes and sassy personality. The pain in my chest is unbearable. It feels like my soul is tearing apart. I couldn't help the tears running down my face even if I tried. I thought back to the three people by the throne, Skylar, Ryder, and Ryder's brother. I guess I don't have to worry about his brother anymore. He would have died soon after I hit him.

"Just two more to go," I say to myself. I push my overwhelming heartbreak aside and concentrate on forming a plan.

Escape. Kill Ryder and Skylar.

Could I actually do it? Kill her? Is that not what she was doing to me today? She was killing me. She showed no remorse when she took his side or any sign of the connection we have when we entered that room. Could I kill her for her betrayal? The truth is I might have to. My face turns into a scowl, feeling anger at myself for a part of me still wanting to protect her. Well, I will deal with that emotional mess when it comes time later. I. Need. To. Get. Out.

I get up and walk around the front of the bars to inspect them. They are all sturdy. Whoever made them that many years ago did a great job. It's unlikely that I will be able to break out through these bars. My best choice is to escape when they move me from the cell. It's closer than I would have liked to my assigned destiny. It also leaves less room for errors.

Testing the stable door to my freedom results in a resigned sigh emitting from me. Confirming that waiting until movement from the cell would be my best option, as I feel my injuries remind me of their protest of my activities.

I take out my phone from my pocket, confirming what I already suspected. It has web cracks all over the front screen. All that kicking and falling didn't just bruise my body. I try to turn on my phone. The electronic screen stares back at me black and unresponsive. Unable to reach out for help seems right on track with what is happening right now. I don't feel too surprised at this, but a small part of me feels defeat. Even if it did work, being several floors down would make it hard to call anyone with reception.

I move back to the bench. The only thing left now is to get some sleep to heal before I have to fight for my life. Literally. Laying down, I take a deep breath to let go of all my anxiety, close my eyes, and drift off.

All I see is black around me, which I am okay with. I relax more, knowing I won't be haunted by Skylar in my dreams tonight. A dreamless night is what I need right now, considering the situation. I then feel the disruption of energy before I see anything. The black around me turns slowly to a medium blue. I feel her hands on my back, wrapping around my mid-section. They feel like they're holding on for dear life. I try to push away from the embrace, feeling stuck, suffocated. Anger rips through me, enabling me to turn around to face her. Her face comes into focus. Her beautiful face and blue eyes. Anger and sadness crash through me.

Grab her. Grab her. Grab her.

I grab her neck. She gives me the saddest smile I have ever seen in my life.

I feel pain, only pain. I can't tell where it is coming from, but I need it to stop. Her face blurs and disappears. The pain slowly stops, allowing the space to turn black again. Everything is still and back to empty. My large emotions moments ago slowly seep back to the fringes. I hear a distant noise—a noise of metal. Wake up Now!

Straight out of sleep, I jump up in a panic to fight as reality comes into full view again. My heart is pounding. I take in the bars in front of me. The door is open with the key in the lock. A slow breath leaves my lips as I compose myself. My wrists still in shackles, I move gingerly around the door to grab the key. As quietly as possible, I move the metal against metal. As the key is released, my eyes are trained as much as possible on the door leaving the room. I try the key on my cuffs. To my dismay, they don't let me get the rest of my freedom.

Okay, so two keys. This barrier is not the worst thing to happen. I just need to get out as quietly as I can with metal cuffs attached to me. I nod to myself in encouragement. I close my eyes and try to envision the route I came in. Opening them, I steel myself to be ready for battle if necessary, but this is a stealth mission. Collecting the extra slack on my cuffs, I quietly move my feet towards the first door to my freedom. I kneel close to the floor for more security as I reach for the door handle. I move the door slowly to be as unnoticeable as possible between two guards. With roughly two inches between the door frame and the heavy mass blocking me, I look out. With the visual I am allowed, I notice a black boot of a guard. To my surprise, he is already lying on the floor. I open the door more to take in the whole scene. Instead of two guards, there is one now on the floor, and the other disappeared

I don't think about it any further and move forward. As close to the wall as possible, my momentum moves me to the next door that holds the first set of stairs. The only lighting I have from torches bouncing off the walls and floor. Each step is careful and persistent to reach my goal: freedom out of this demented house. As I reach the top of the first staircase, I immediately notice there is no opposition waiting for me.

Figuring out which doors to go through is slightly an issue. I find a closet or two of random things. But the main problem will be the open throne room and the hallways between that room and the front door. If I were these manic people, I would be concerned about a possible threat from above and not below. Especially since apparently the most considerable threat is supposed to be locked in a fortified cage.

The doorway to the throne room didn't have an actual door to it. As soon as I go through it, I will be vulnerable to whatever lies in its large and vast corners. Getting to this point feels like hours of life. If I don't stay focused, I will run out of time. Stealth mode requires a lot of patience and time. And it isn't exactly like I have the luxury of a clock at the ready for me.

I have two options in this great hall: stay against the wall like I have been doing or use the room's pillars for cover. Because of the size of it, there's less light for visual aid. I decide, swiftly moving through the doorway towards my fate.

I start against the wall until coming to the first pillar, moving to go against the large marble mass and pause. I glance around the room, and there are several doors anyone can come out of at any moment. I take several breaths to assess any noise or movement in this large space with me. At a fast walk, my legs move me through the gap to the next pillar. The main double doors I need to get to are located three pillars away. The closest torches on the walls and pillars flicker, throwing my shadow with each movement that I make.

I move to the next one. Once again, pausing to listen to anything that will indicate an alert to me moving around. It's silent except for the small noise of the flickering embers around me. Keep going. Time is running out. I push forward against the two remaining pillars closest to the large wooden doors. Just like before, I move lower to the floor and slowly move the door open several inches.

There I am met with the end of my luck as I spot moving shadows on the floor and wall. One silhouette is moving towards the door, and one is moving away. I wait to watch the person closest to the door. They stop before it, then turn around. They appear to be in rotations. The next guard that comes near the entrance is when I will go out. The only thing on my side right now is the element of surprise. The figure comes close to the door again and stops. That's when I push on it with all my strength to smash them in the face. The guard yells out in pain. I now have a clear view of two other guards blocking my way to the other side of the hallway.

They look at me wide-eyed in surprise. The shock is shortlived, with the two guards jumping into action. They stand next to each other. One of the guards yells "Breach" before taking out his sword and bringing up his shield.

The guard I hit with the door is vulnerable, so I go for him first. He has blood running down his face as he tries to grab his dagger from his waistband. His hands are slick with blood from holding them to his face. I kick his hand away, clutching his head, and slam the side of it into the wall. He slumps down to the floor like a rag doll. The other two make a barrier, putting both of their shields up next to each other. It's not giving me a lot of space to hit them with an attack, which is the point.

The only plan of action available is the direct kind. Pushing my body forward in a burst of speed, I propel myself as fast as I can towards them. They look prepared for my attack, unflinching from the speed coming at them.

They are wrong.

I jump right before running directly against the shieldbearer on the left. The foot's force and weight in the middle of his shield push him back and to the floor. As I move with the man falling, it puts me parallel to the other one. I lean back slightly, getting my shackle chains around his neck, and flip him as hard as I can. He lands on his stomach on the floor, his shield away from him. He doesn't get back up.

The guy whose shield I kicked now has a dent where my foot landed. He sees his fallen comrade and gets up in a frenzy. He starts yelling at me, grabbing his weapon to charge me. He is clumsy and executing his attack poorly. My body moves with practice allowing me to dodge his advances with ease. With all the dodging, I work to be behind him, ending with him in a headlock. He struggles in my grip, trying to hit me with his weapon, but the angle just isn't right. He hits the floor like dead weight like the first one.

I look towards the heavy double doors to see if anyone else is coming to attack me. That fight was a lot of noise. If they aren't here now, they are on their way. Literally, as I think that, I feel a sharp object against the back of my neck.

There's a guard at the top of the stairs I missed.

Annoyance runs through me at working so hard to get this far and being caught. It's insulting to my skill set. My cuffed hands are raising into the air soon after to help convince whoever is behind me that I'm helpless, regardless of the bodies lying around me.

"You almost escaped successfully," he whispers in my ear. It's a voice that I know but can't place, putting me on edge. He grabs the back of my shirt and throws me against the wall. I get to see the face of my attacker, justifying my feeling of uneasiness. I see the face of the weird creepy guy who tried to steal the older woman's taxi and attacked me the first time in the street.

I grow angry when I realize that he is the start of everything that has happened to me. That one interaction with him caused a ripple effect to this moment. "He will be excited to talk to you" is what he said to me that night. He meant Ryder.

I give him a death glare as he holds me in place against the wall with his left palm, which is firmly placed right below my neck. He quickly produces a short sword to wrap up my slack in the chains, effectively disabling the use of my hands. He has blood on him, the front of his shirt, and some on his face. There is a deep cut on the top of the forearm holding the sword, potentially to the bone. The blood on his shirt looks like he tried to, at one point, wrap his arm in his shirt to stop the bleeding.

His eyes are unfocused; he is sweaty and is breathing hard. The kind of aura he's giving is the kind found with wild animals that will attack just because you are near-by. When seen on a person, their actions are without emotion, conscience, or thought.

"What should I do with you? I could return you to the cell and wait several hours for Ryder to kill you," he uses the flat side of his sword still wrapped in chains to hit my cheek, "Or I could kill you now and say you died in battle. Just to be done with it."

His surprise jump on me caused my reactionary skills to pause, which cause me to be confined. Now, the only point of attack left, while this psycho talks to himself, is head butting or kicking him. They both have low chances of working in my favor. I need him to let go of the sword and free up my hands. I feel my window of opportunity dwindling. My instinct decides for me by head butting him in the nose. He stumbles but doesn't fully let go of his stance as I hoped, shaking his head to gain clarity.

He growls, pushing me on the wall harder and putting his sword point to my neck, "I think I am going to kill you. You are way more trouble than you are worth, even if you are the last royal bloodline."

Chapter: 23

My eyes snap to his when he says this to me. He immediately notices the action.

His response doesn't hide his smugness, "Oh, yes. Since you are about to die, I'll just tell you. You are so important to everyone here because you are the last of your royal bloodline. Your family has ruled over us for hundreds of years. Until Ryder's father rebelled and killed your family."

I push against him even with the sword against my throat, "My Uncle…"

He cuts off what I'm about to say with a deep chested laugh, causing blood to go into his mouth, making his teeth red, "Your Uncle! What a joke. The man that raised you is not your Uncle! He was the captain of the guard! Your father's right-hand man. Who took you and raised you as his own. You are the last…and now you aren't."

● ● ●

He starts to push the point further into my neck. I can feel liquid on the right side of my shirt.

What was happening just moments before is gone. My eyes and mind could no longer see the madman putting a sword into my throat in a hallway. My mind transports, propelling me back to a time I didn't think I remembered.

I'm standing in a room that I don't know. I'm stuck in a position near the back corner. From what I see, this room is beautiful and filled with different crisp colors—golds and dark browns cover expensive looking chairs, tables, and sofas. On the tables are silver trays. Some of them are holding pink and purple flowers in a white vase. Maroon, dark green, and beige color the walls with flowing designs. There's an area rug under the main sitting sofa range that is an assortment of maroons in a beautiful design.

Ignoring the beautiful room, I stand looking at what has my full attention: the three people standing next to the sitting range, talking amongst themselves.

There are two men and one woman. The woman has her back to me with brown wavy hair to her shoulders, a light pink rose-colored dress, and flat-heeled shoes. To her right, the man has short brown hair, dressed in a black suit with a green striped tie, stands closest to the woman. The other man has short black hair, appears to have a goatee', and is wearing all black.

The men discuss something I can't hear, but their hand gestures show that it's severe. Then, the black-hair man grabs a dagger from near his foot and goes towards the door embedded into the wall. The man with the brown hair yells, "Stop!" the other's advance to the door stops immediately and turns to look at the pair. The face is Uncle's but younger. The woman whispers in the man's ear next to her with her hand fondly resting on his chest. The brown-hair man nods his head at the woman, moving in front of the man I know as my Uncle.

He points to me and says with authority, "Liam, I know this is a difficult time, and hard decisions need to be made. But you need to protect her." Uncle doesn't move or say anything. The man grabs the front of Uncle's shirt by his neck collar, "You do everything you can to keep her safe. She is the only priority. She is how we survive this; that is an order. Do you understand me?"

Uncle nods his head, silently putting away his weapon. There is shouting on the other side of the door. The three of them look at the door at the same time. Uncle then runs to me and picks me up as if I weigh nothing. I feel tears running down my face.

The woman runs over to me, kissing me on my forehead. Her face is glistening with tears herself, "We love you, Selena, always. No matter where we are or what you're doing. We will be there with you."

The other man comes up behind her to pull her away from us. Before he does, he puts his hand on my cheek to rub it with his thumb, a sad smile on his face. He whispers to Uncle, "Go now before they see you."

⁂

We can hear banging against the door. Uncle grabs a blanket from a nearby chair to cover me. Before he puts it over me, the last thing I see is my parents standing in the spot they were before, facing the door. They stand there together with the woman's arm through the man's in confidence, patiently waiting for the door to come bursting open. Then I see black, nothingness. What I feel is sadness, confusion, and anger filling me.

I hear screaming.

Reality comes crashing back in. My eyes refocus on what's happening in front of me, a very different scene from moments before. The screaming I heard just seconds ago is still happening. It's coming from the man who was about to kill me. He's now lying on the floor, holding the arm previously inhibiting my escape against the wall. The arm is burnt entirely black. His weapon is now lying on the floor near him. Directly next to the cuffs that were previously on my wrists. The sections of my skin that once touched on the metal now show empty spaces.

Trying to figure out what happened, my eyes go to my wrists. Green flames are radiating off of my forearms and open palms. The green flames licking my skin never cause me pain; they feel warm but never hot. My right-hand goes to the spot where this man was intent on bleeding me out. The bleeding has stopped, and now scar tissue took its place over the cut. Moving my vision line to encompass the surrounding corridor hallway I'm still in; all the torch flames are now green. The green light is now mingling with the red walls and floorboards. In fact, the main throne room farther in the distance also has a green hue to it.

"You stupid bitch!" the favorite guard of my enemy spits at me from the floor. My head quickly turns back to him, lying on the floor with his wound on one arm and the other burnt. My anger flares at this sorry excuse of a human being before me.

This anger is compounded by the betrayal of Skylar, Ryder, the man in front of me, and not knowing the truth of my life's secrets. Everything I know is a lie. With my anger raging, the fires lining the wall increase with it.

Bending down, I pick up his weapon that's on the floor in front of me. I walk the short distance between us and point it at his throat, "Listen, guard dog, you do not get to be upset at me for trying to survive. You are just upset because you didn't get what you wanted and got injured. I am not a pawn in other people's games! I am a person with feelings and a life. I am here, and I will stay!"

I'm having a hard time controlling my emotional anger. The urge to kill this man is overwhelming. There's already been so much destruction, but would the world be worse with him gone?

My fingers grip the handle harder. I distribute my weight, bringing my right foot back, and kicking him in the face. His face lolls to the side, indicating he's out cold. I don't immediately remove the weapon from his throat, having not fully committed to a decision.

● ● ●

Then I feel it. The energy around me alters.

Warm, feminine hands are on my upper shoulders, moving to my neck in a calming manner. They move from my neck to either side of my face, rubbing on my cheeks in a loving circular motion.

From behind me, I hear her whisper in reassurance, the voice I dream about often, "It's okay, Selena." I don't say anything. I don't move. For a second, I stay in her welcoming embrace, accepting it and letting it soothe me temporarily.

She moves her hands from my face to my arms, right before the flames start. I feel her moving forward to have her essence and weight against my back fully. She slowly moves her hands down my arms, where I feel her calmness and see the blue coming off of her. My green flames mix with her blue, making a turquoise color, the fire slowly dwindling. The flames are soon gone from my being, and the torches are back to the standard hue once again.

Skylar whispers again in my ear, "You need to leave. Now." She removes her hands from my skin, pushing against my back toward the staircase. I stumble along with her push but continue to move to the spiral stairs. Before I round the spiral column, I spare a glance in her direction. Skylar is running quietly in the opposite direction back into the belly of the beast, trying her best not to be seen. Until this moment, I never knew someone could feel so empty and grateful at the same time.

* * *

I move quickly up the last set of stairs I honestly ever want to see in my life, moving in a light jog through to the last hallway to my freedom. Freedom to regroup my life as I know it. I abruptly stop jogging when I see the butler standing by the front door. My hand is holding the weapon still. With certainty, at least to Gregory, I'm the picture of a mess.

He appears to give it minimal thought before reaching for the door handle of the front door. Gregory opens it stepping back to allow me space to pass him. In his position, he put his right hand across his chest towards his shoulder and bows slightly. I don't know what he's doing, but I'm not looking a gift horse in the mouth, moving through the distance quickly.

When I approach him, he bows, "Majesty, you may want to hide the sword in the public eye, ma'am."

I just absent-mindedly nod my head, barely registering what he is saying but looking around my body to figure out where to put it. The only thing I can think to do is put it down my pants against my thigh, with my shirt over the hilt. It's a good thing it isn't a full-length sword.

As I pass him, I acknowledge him in parting,
"Gregory."

I hurry as fast as I can down the front steps to the sidewalk. I'm taking a deep breath, registering that I made it out of that hell somehow.

The sun is just starting to rise above the horizon, with its joyful yellow rays of hope showing a new day. For me, it's representing many new things. I'm not sure if I want to love or hate the metaphor or the actual scene presenting itself to me. Think about this later. Step one, I need to get to safety. I start my journey to Uncle's shop. There is a lot we have to discuss.

The route I take to Uncle's shop is different from usual, in case they know how I travel. I arrive at the building later than I want, but it's better than not arriving at all. Everything part of my body is exhausted and hurting by the time I get there. My walking strides are not as wide or fast because of the hidden sword. I'm using more energy to get myself from one place to another.

The lights are off in the store, the sun is barely just rising, and the shop isn't open yet. Uncle should be upstairs eating breakfast. I got the key to unlock the door. As I put it in its designated home, the door pushes open slightly. This simple action stops all my movement. I look through the glass into the store to see if I notice anything out of the ordinary. There is no movement of any people inside, but some of the back shelves are tipped over. I gently pull the sword out of its hiding place, holding it ready. I push the front door open with my shoulder, stepping past the threshold. I'm looking for indicators of what happened.

Several shelves on the floor have products scattered around, broken and smashed. As I get closer, my shoes start making the sound of cracking glass. Looking at the register area, I see the glass case that the register sits on is almost entirely in pieces. Behind the register, the candles that sit around the Buddha statue are still softly glowing from the night before. I take in the view of the entire back of the store from where I'm standing. Both the doors to the back-training room and the upstairs were slightly ajar and appear to be broken.

My mind jumps back to the fight several hours before with the man who tried to cut my throat. He came from the stairs leading to the front door and visibly had blood on his shirt and face that didn't belong to him. He must have just arrived back from a mission.

My heart sinks. Please, no, please don't be what I think it is.

I stay silent and unmoving for the next several seconds to listen to any suspicious noises that I need to investigate first. There is nothing. My sprinting speed kicks in, launching me off the glass, taking me to the upstairs living quarters. My eyes search around the room before my body is entirely up the case of stairs.

The space I grew up in with the man who owned this building was in complete disarray. Drawers are in disorder, showing emptied contents all over the floor. Pillows and cushions are torn, stuffing hanging out. Kitchenware is either smashed into pieces or thrown around. I make quick work looking around each room. With the state of everything, it is clear someone was up here looking for something. They noticeably didn't find it. Everything that is happening or has happened has no time to register in my mind. Uncle isn't up here, and I need to see him.

❊ ❊ ❊

Then I hear it—a thudding from downstairs, from the area of the training room.

Chapter: 24

I run down the stairs to the training room door, sword out, and push it further open. Quickly my eyes take in the scene.

A gasp leaves my mouth. There is a weapon near the wall closest to the door. Uncle is leaning on a sword to stand, looking a bit worn down but alive. When his eyes realize it's me, relief floods his face. He tries to rush over to me, but he clearly has a leg injury. I drop my sword on the floor, rushing to him.

I hug him hard, feeling tears coming to the edges of my eye quickly. Uncle flinches but still wraps his protective arms around me as tightly as his injuries would let him.

"I thought you died! This place is a mess." I state through my elevated emotions.

His one hand rubs my back to reassure me the best he can. "And I thought you died, but we are both here now," his response comes along with a raspy voice.

I look up to see bruising on his throat. Whatever happened here must have been a huge fight. Obviously, he suffered a small blow to his vocal cords during it.

"I had a great teacher, so I won," I say, wiping several of the tears that fall down my face.

His eyes fall upon my newly made scar from several hours ago. I can see a new emotion go through him. It's an energy that can be felt. His feelings and demeanor give me a sense that his opinion about me has been altered from this second going forward.

"Of course you won. You are your father's daughter. You are a survivor," he proudly states.

Tears return to my eyes from this simple statement. At this moment, it feels like a validation given to me that I was unaware I needed to hear. There's so much to say, to ask, to express. My mouth opens to respond to him.

"You kept me safe all these years. I survived because of you. I'm so sorry…"

Before the rest of the words can leave my mouth, there is a banging noise from the front door. Uncle nods for me to go. I swiftly move to pick up my sword. I hear her before I see her.

"What happened here?" a panicking question reaches my ears. Melanie enters my vision as I clear the doorway separating us.

"Selena? Wha…?" Concern and confusion are laced over her face and through her voice. My tired eyes are on Melanie standing in the shop, holding three cups in a carrier. She's more concentrating on the destruction of the store than me right now. The pause in her questioning gives me time to think over my options of what I will say to her.

I don't have it in me to tell a story, hide, or keep secrets. Right now isn't a time to keep anything from anyone, especially someone who has always accepted me as I am. I hope after I tell Melanie the truth, she remains that way.

Melanie sets her eyes on me, her full attention making me feel like a mess under her gaze. I try to reassure her, "Everyone is okay; just someone broke in and trashed the store."

"Are you sure everyone okay? Is that blood? Did you call the police? Do I need to call the police? Are you holding a sword?" With every question that Melanie asks, her voice sounds more nervous than the last.

"We are taking care of it and will be involving the police," revisiting the cups in her hand, "What is that for?"

She looks at the cups in her hand too, briefly forgotten, "Your Uncle asked me to surprise you this morning for breakfast so we could all hang out. So, I picked up some coffee."

"Melanie, I don't deserve you as a friend. You have always been supportive and honest with me. I couldn't have asked for a better person in my life." Even with everything that is in front of her right now, her concern is for us.

"Thanks?" she answers with more of a question than gratitude, still displaying a small smile.

"We need to take care of all of this right now. I am going to help Uncle sort this out. Can you wait up in the apartments for me? Then I can explain everything to you."

Melanie looks around the store again, then back at me, squinting her eyes, "Everything, everything?"

I couldn't help but smile at her mild suspicious behavior, "Yes, everything."

"Alright," she answers, drawing out the word. Melanie starts walking to the door to the stairs going up, then pivots around, putting down the coffee, "You guys are going to need this more than me right now."

"Appreciated," pausing to think, then yelling after her, "By the way, it is a mess up there too."

"Of course it is. Explaining everything, right?" Melanie asks, raising her voice to reach me.

"Yes," I respond with certainty. Melanie waves her hand at me in a carefree manner.

With Melanie out of view, a hand goes on my shoulder for reassurance. I turn to look at Uncle. He is still using a sword to put some of his weight onto, holding him up.

"It is time to tell her," I state to him. He continues looking at me, listening to what needs to be said, "She has known less than me but has been behind me every step of the way, as much as you. I'm going to tell her about me."

He nods his head in understanding, "I think that she was ready to hear it before today. But yes, she deserves to know." He pauses before adding, "Just like you do. It is time to lay everything out in the open."

I look into the eyes of the man who raised me and began explaining everything weighing on me before he can, "Two days ago, I had a conversation with you about being alone in life. I told you I didn't want to be alone because of my differences from other people. So, I started dating. Both of the people I dated turned out to be untrustworthy. And the woman I loved betrayed me and broke my heart. Which is how I got captured in the first place."

Uncle looks at me sympathetically, rubbing my back, "I'm sorry your heart is broken, and you had to experience that. It will be okay. Maybe not today, but later it will be okay." He is saying it in a way that makes me feel like it's to both of us.

I take a deep breath before starting the real conversation, "Last night, when I was captured, I found out you weren't my uncle by blood. You were my parent's security guard or general. You saved my life from their fate and promised to keep me safe from the people that did this to us."

As the words left my mouth, there is a deep sadness that reaches him. It's showing just under the surface, something he has had to live with for so long in secret.

He answers in an apologetic tone, "I know this information must be tough for you. This situation is not how I wanted you to find out. Even though I'm not your Uncle by blood, I was named your God Father at your birth for one of these reasons. Your father was my best friend and king. It was decided a long time ago if something like what happened came to be, that I would save you if that were the only way. Out of the three of us, there always needed to be one of us to help you in life."

I asked quickly, needing more, "Why did they both stay that night? Why didn't one leave with us to escape from the people attacking?"

"Your parents knew what was at risk making that decision. They stayed together to allow us time to get away to hide in safety. If only one of them were in the room, the rebels would have split up looking for the other. It happened very quickly, and there was not a lot of time to act or plan. Both of your parents staying in the room was to stall for time, allowing us to exit the grounds. This action left the rebels looking for a small child hiding in the rooms within the house. Not outside."

That isn't the response I thought he was going to say. But it makes perfect sense, especially from a warrior standpoint.

It still hurt my heart for the pair of people that loved me most in the world to self-sacrifice like that.

"I don't know what to do. I have lost everything in one day. A psychopath is hunting me, people I love were taken from me, and my life as I know it has changed. I don't know where to go from here."

The answer I receive from my statement doesn't come from either one of us. It comes from another female voice from behind us, "You regroup, and you rise."

Uncle's eyes are no longer on me but on the person behind me, "Took you long enough."

I turn around to see who took it upon themselves to enter this very private moment. My eyes take in the face of Abigale. My mind flashes back to the work party I was invited to by Ryder. To when I was leaving, and Abigale nodded to me.

Abigale is currently looking at Uncle, smiling softly.

"Nice to see you too, Liam. It has been awhile. We were trying to get here faster but had to be careful. We came as quickly as we could," she answers his accusation. She, like both of us, looks tired and worn down.

Abigale is looking directly at me now with a severe look. She repeats it for me, "You regroup, and you rise," She puts her right hand in a fist across her chest to her left shoulder, as Gregory did at the house, and bows slightly, "Your Majesty."

When she does this, it makes me feel slightly uncomfortable. When Gregory did it, I was trying to leave and didn't pay him much attention. With Abigale does it, it makes everything more a reality.

"How am I supposed to rise against the resources he has at his disposal? When I barely got out of that building with my life?" I ask.

"With help," Abigale answers as she moves back to gesture to the space inside the store.

I move more into the area but not too far from the training room. Uncle moves to stand to my right and Abigale on my left. Several people's silhouettes are scattering across the shop with us. Most of whom I know. There is Gregory, who I recently had the pleasure of meeting, my high school counselor, my boss Joe, and I think that is my neighbor near the corner. They all put their right hand in a fist across their chest to their left shoulder and bow. I look at Abigale in surprise.

"I told you at the party. You will always find allies in the unlikeliest of places."

Uncle smiles and waves at Joe. He reciprocates the same to him. Abigale has a tight smile in response to their interaction but elects not to comment on it.

She looks back to me, grabbing my attention with her voice, "There are others, but they can't be here right now."

I ask the only question that really mattered, "Why?"

Abigale seems surprised at the simplicity of my reaction, "Why what?"

"Why does it matter if I fight or run away, never to have to deal with this again?"

Before answering, she looks around the room at the others, "[It was] your destiny to lead our people from the beginning. But it's your right to walk away if you want. Then we will continue to exist as we are now, with nothing changing. The choice is yours. No one will make it for you."

"Does it matter which family is leading really? If Ryder and his family make everyone successful, why change it?" I ask, listing my questions.

Abigale responds calmly, "You are correct. Ryder's family has brought wealth to several people but at what cost? How he treated you is how we know him except for a select few. He rules with fear and tricks."

"How am I supposed to choose when I don't even know who I am?"

She tilts her head slightly to the side taking me in, "Yes, you do. You don't know the history or several important facts about what happened, but that doesn't define who you are. Liam and I can fill in the blanks. But you know who you are. You are brave, you help people in need, you do the right thing, and you don't allow others to step all over you. You are Selena Wilson."

Uncle speaks up, "Selena, she is right. You can leave and never have to worry about this again. Or you can stay to fight to protect people to make sure something like this," he motions to his store, "never happens again."

I look around, taking in everything they are saying. An internal battle is raging inside of me, a flight or fight. Glancing at Abigale, she is looking at Uncle. Her face barely gives anything away, but she seems incredibly sad.

What has happened, and is happening now, is affecting more than myself. Looking at Joe and the rest of the group's faces more closely, I see an underlying pain. If I left now, this pain that resides in this group of humans, my people, will continue to remain there. Uncle didn't raise me to leave people in pain when they need my support the most. I have to accept that this is bigger than just me or a history of what happened. This choice has to do with a diverse group of people suffering as much as I have. I must accept that my decision affects everyone else around me too. I may not be able to take their past pain away, but I can certainly try to make it less in the future.

"What would you like to do?"

I look into Abigale's eyes with determination, "We rise."

After agreeing to change my life for many unknown others, I leave the group behind to figure out the next immediate steps for our safety.

Uncle and Abigale discuss how both our side and Ryder's are too busy scrambling to recover from the night's events to make any moves. Everyone is just trying to make sense of what happened.

Taking two of the still warm cups with me, I make my way to my waiting friend a level above me in what's an alarmingly destroyed living space. Everyone's voice behind me slowly fades. I fill with a feeling I'm familiar with, but not to this degree.

That feeling is grief, and it's overwhelming.

Before climbing the stairs, I close my eyes and lean on the wall to feel its hovering presence over my heart. The point of taking this second to myself is not to pinpoint the leading cause but to greet its existence. To say hello to my wandering companion. It can be from my lost lover, from a previous life gone, from the loss of my ability to make decisions solely for myself, or from the places I love no longer being safe.

What I do know is that grief is the feeling of loss from something personally being taken away. It's a presence being removed from a way of life. That presence can be an object, a person, a memory, a feeling, something that causes comfort.

There are known stages of grief that come in waves. These waves can be small or crash into you, overwhelming the senses.

The senses will feel abandoned, an emptiness, almost like a black hole taking the light out of the area. When the wave hits, it is like all the happiness you may have been feeling a moment before is gone, replaced with intense pain or aching. But suppressing the feeling will only stump the healing process.

Society doesn't always allow the space to express or show the feelings these waves create—the sense of grief portrayed as something fixable by a hug, a smile, or happiness. Human emotions are meant to change frequently. Feeling sadness or grief of loss is normal.

Any amount of happiness may temporarily be able to relieve the main feeling. But at the end of everything, when no one else is around, there is no one to get you out of that pit. The unending aching of something being taken. What is the solution? How do you fix it by yourself?

Acceptance.

Acceptance of what happened, of how you feel, of things out of your control. Acceptance that not everyone around you will understand your choices. Acceptance that not everyone will be on the same page as you and differences will happen. Transform that acceptance and those feelings into something positive to give yourself and the world.

These emotions flood me and wrap me in their warm embrace. What has happened, happened. What is lost is already lost. Looking up the stairs, I look onwards to my new destiny. With grief and acceptance in my heart, I make my step forward.
The only thing left is to keep moving forward.

Acknowledgment

This book means everything to me from start to finish. But it means more because of the supportive people that were behind me while making it. On the days I wanted to light everything on fire, these individuals steadied my hand in reassurance.

Firstly, I would like to thank my wife, Kristen Stitt. Thank you for giving me space to rant, bounce ideas off out loud, and have hyper-focused goals and mental breakdowns. For reading early drafts, edits, and giving me the hard truths. I couldn't have asked for a better partner to have during this.

Additionally, many thanks go out to Tatianna Mason. You helped me in many ways that aren't fully seen. First and foremost, you literally told me not to light anything on fire while I was angry. Secondly, when I was at my worst, you were there helping me through whatever it was at the time. I appreciate you!

An additional thanks go to my parents, James Heidt and Jo-Ann Messer. You both provided insurmountable support and helped me along with the process in different ways. Both your excitement and reminders not to give up were a beacon during the dark days of writing.

Here's a special shout out to my friends at Only Human. You guys never hesitated on jumping in to help with questions or guidance. With a direct thank you to TK LaFleur. You were the closest thing to a mentor I had during this process. You answered every question, gave a lot of supportive encouragement, and provided the different platforms I could work with.

A special thank you to Gillian Slocum-Ross. I know you said to write it out, I'm sure this wasn't what you meant, but it turned out to be fantastic. You provided a safe place, and I am grateful.

A huge thank you to Kyle Paige and Brianna Fredriksen. This book made it to the finish line because of the help and effort on your part. This story would have looked a lot different than it did today. Bri, you work wonders. I will be forever grateful for you being my editor.

Here's to you, David Messer. I know if you were here, you would be very proud of me.

About The Author

Rebecca grew up in New York and Pennsylvania. She lived previously in Colorado and New Mexico. She graduated with a Bachelor's from Excelsior College. For many years, Rebecca worked a career in Management within the Restaurant Industry and worked with the Financial spectrum for a time. She is finding her way back to her true passion for History, Art, and Writing. Doing this allowed Rebecca to write her first book, Acceptance: The Beginning.

She wrote the first installment of the Acceptance books to help deal with the evolving situation of Quarantine and hard life hurtles. This book allowed her the platform to turn the falling world outside and inside her home into something positive. Rebecca now lives with her wife Kristen and their two dogs, a Husky and an Akita, and their cats. Rebecca is currently writing the follow-up Acceptance: The Reality.